THE GHOSTS
OF
EVERBRIDGE MANOR

KEVIN J. HACKETT

ISBN (Paperback): 979-8605532125

ALSO BY KEVIN J. HACKETT

Life Among the Dead

Prologue

L enore stood in the front garden amidst the trampled rosemary bushes. Behind her, the dark expanse of Everbridge Manor loomed, bounded from below by fog and from above by muddy grey skies. The stone pathway before her led out toward the manor's open entrance gate, with the Everbridge beyond, spanning a wide river. The bridge was unimpressive, despite its grand name. Upstream to the left, on the far side of the river, she could see the town of River's Edge, ominous black smoke roiling above it in two columns, as if some fires were burning there.

She walked over to the vegetable patch where some green beans and carrots grew. There was an old scarecrow posted in the patch, rising up larger than a large man. His mouth was a thick, crooked stitch made from black yarn; his eyes were large, irregular circles, filled in with the same yarn. The scarecrow wore one of The Master's old straw hats, faded to colorlessness from a sun that seemed to have ceased to exist, except on rare, exquisite occasions when it made a brief appearance. Ages ago, she had built and installed this scarecrow herself to keep crows from the green beans and carrots. It had long since abdicated that job in favor of less useful types of hauntings. It had to go.

She pulled the scarecrow from the garden, dragged its bulk to an empty patch of dirt—there were many—and soaked it with kerosene from a house lantern. As she worked, she noticed the crosshatch stitches of the eyes that went in all directions; she had always been a far better gardener than seamstress. She struck a match on the scarecrow's post and set the whole kit to blaze. The birds would not show up, she knew, but if they did, they could have the beans.

She was wearing her town clothes, selected some time ago to appease The Master for an impromptu visit to River's Edge: a stiff grey blouse with a single-button lace collar, a charcoal-colored, full skirt, and a beige sweater with elaborate, embroidered flowers. This outfit was uncomfortable and impractical and held only bad memories. She wished to never wear it again. Standing beside the burning scarecrow pile, she stripped down to her undergarments and threw the town clothes into the flames.

Lenore next regarded the nearby garden axe, its hilt wedged into its old life-partner, the battered oak tree stump. The axe was often a problem, but she knew she couldn't throw it into the river; it was needed for chopping wood. Besides, sometimes things that were disposed of showed back up around the manor when she least cared to revisit them.

She left the burning scarecrow, town clothes, and axe where they all were and went inside. She was on her way upstairs to select something to wear that was comfortable and denim and had pantlegs, when she remembered her book.

There were many books on tall shelves throughout the manor, most of which were far too boring to ever bother reading. In a shelf beside the stairway, she found the large, dusty, brown book she had last been working on: a collection of the writings of Platonicus. It was musty, in both content and appearance. Above her, someone walked slowly across the landing upstairs, muttering quietly. Lenore found the page in Platonicus where she had left off and regarded it for a minute, standing in the front entry still wearing only her undergarments. She noted, with some sadness, that she was nearly done with the current page, and in fact, the whole book. Soon she would need to select another...one more unpleasant business in a house where there was no shortage of them. She marked her place and put Platonicus back up on the shelf. She did not plan to return to him for at least three more months.

At the sideboard of the parlor, she checked to be sure her Grand-daddy's rifle was still propped against the wall. It was there as she had expected, along with two bullets standing nearby, pointing straight up on their flat ends. The gun was a last resort, but Lenore needed to know it was available should things ever get so bad that the ending power of a firearm was needed. It *had* been needed before.

As she went up the stairway, she came up to the extravagant portrait of himself that The Master had commissioned some years earlier. It was supposed to show him off as a towering, powerful pillar of his community and his home, but Lenore thought the whole rendering was ridiculous. He was a merchant in a small town, wearing a paisley ascot and a silk waistcoat and holding his stomach in while sitting behind his giant mahogany desk, surrounded by busy ledgers. It was painted with marginal skill in the style of the portraits of ancient kings. The artist's interpretation, Lenore believed, only emphasized The Master's roundness and small, mean eyes. Earlier that day, she had pulled it down from its hook, badly ripping one of the corners of the canvas. Now, she regarded it for a moment and hung it back up, ignoring its damage.

Up in her bedroom, she regarded herself in the tall mirror and winced. She had some bruises on her face, but they would heal in time. She found some practical clothes to wear and dressed while thinking about the remaining jobs that needed to be done. Some furniture needed to be moved from upstairs to downstairs, so she started there.

TWO DAYS LATER, a horse strode across the Everbridge, its male rider slumped forward across the beast's neck and mane. The morning was cold and dark; it would rain later in the day.

The man was not truly *riding* the horse, as he was barely conscious. Instead, it was more that he had been draped across the mount like a blanket thrown on a sofa such that it barely balances. His upper arm and shoulder were tangled in the reins, which is really what kept him from falling off the horse altogether. His mouth hung open; she could see his smeared red teeth. Also, he had recently been bleeding from the eyes and ears, though they had begun to crust over.

Lenore approached and took the horse's bridle, examining the man for a moment. He was about her own age, which was just 30. He wore black trousers and riding boots, a beige shirt, and a black suit coat with one of the shoulder seams ripped open. The man was handsome, though that was hard to tell at that moment with his swollen cheeks and puffy eyes. He had recently been in a fight which he had not won. His injuries were grave, but Lenore believed she could tend to them.

The saddle had the horse's name branded into it in small, ornate letters: "His Majesty." She led His Majesty closer to the front of Everbridge Manor, saying to the man, "Oh you poor dear. Such a mess." She wiped some of the blood from his face, from his eyes in particular, but he could barely open them to see her. His body spasmed through some weak, moist coughs, and he squinted up at her and asked, "Kitty?"

"No, my love," she said. "I'm Lenore."

She untangled the reins from his arm, and tried her best to slip him down from the saddle. He was a tall, fit man with wide shoulders, but Lenore was strong enough to manage his weight. The awkwardness of the height and the dead weight of his body complicated matters, though, so he slipped and fell the last six inches, sprawling flat on the stones in front of the manor. He grunted from the impact. "I'm so sorry, Sunshine," she said as she rolled him onto a blankct that she had brought from inside the house.

Lenore dragged him over the entry landing and down the long downstairs hallway, speaking quietly to him as she pulled him toward the low bed prepared in the back bedroom. "You can rest back here. I'll help you."

John & Lenore

For a long time, every one of John's senses failed him. When he managed to open his eyes, there was only darkness beyond. The idea that he might be blind was disconcerting to him, but he could seldom concentrate long enough to think about it. All sound came to him as if he were underwater, muffled and muted. When his nose worked at all, the only odor he could discern was a uniform oily smell; if someone had told him that the whole world outside his body was being fried in a pan, he would have easily believed it. Where it wasn't numb, his skin buzzed.

He came to realize that someone was tending to him – a woman. Her touch was tender, when he could focus on it through the pain, but her treatment was agonizing. Hours and days passed as she repeatedly slathered some kind of burning paste on the top and back of his skull. His injuries were severe, yet he had absolutely no recollection of how he had gotten them.

The bandage-changing and sponging and awkward sips of

water from a spoon and painful unguents made his thoughts swirl back to his days on and around the battlefield. It was sometimes difficult for him to tell what was a vivid recollection of his time as a militia-man, and what was a consequence of being treated for a grave head-wound. He tried to speak on occasion, but the woman gently touched his mouth to silence him.

Once he dreamed that he was on the far side of Eastern Ridge, again fighting in the Battle of the Grey and the Green. His time in the militia was distinguished neither by great bravery nor great cowardice; he had simply been lucky a few key times. Nothing had taught him more about the random nature of life than being a soldier, where fate's coin-flip could easily mean death today or digging graves for your fallen comrades tomorrow. When he stood in formation on the right side of the company commander, those militiamen standing on the left were assigned to take a forward position in a skirmish that ended badly for all of those chosen. He was out on the relative safety of a routine patrol when an ambush back at the camp claimed many lives. And he was well over the Eastern Ridge when his division was attacked from behind, again to severe losses. His dreams were extremely vivid, more like re-enactments than the hazy, jumbled recollections that made up most dreams. He was *there*, back in the damp, grey uniform, cold and confused, shuffling back up some fateful rise toward the inevitable sight of carnage on the other side. When the woman roughly tightened his bandages, he was yanked, gasping, out of the troubling visions.

Eventually, his ears started to pick up sounds, most notably the ticking of a large standing clock nearby. It was in the hall in front of his room. During one long night, he thought he heard the breathing and quiet nickering and hoof-scrapes of a horse, literally there in the room with him! His eyesight was returning, but it was still dark all around. He wasn't well enough to move from the bed, so he could do nothing but lay in discomfort until the woman returned in the morning and revealed with her lamp that there was no livestock nearby.

John's senses slowly returned as the pain in his head lessened, though it was sometimes hard to believe them. A horse, in the room with him, complete with the smell of a barn? Nonsense. The low droning in his ears diminished, revealing other sounds in the area. Sometimes there were whispers coming from the hallway, sometimes someone in the house was shouting or laughing, sometimes there was a barely-audible crying, and sometimes there came the sound of plates or pans smashing. A few times, it sounded like someone was *very* nearby, scraping a spoon against the bottom of a tin can. The clock ticked the seconds away, though occasionally it fell eerily silent. *Everything* now smelled like kerosene, but sometimes, in the dark of the night, he would get a whiff of fruit nearby, too...maybe peaches.

The cluttered room had one door and no windows, as far as he could tell. In addition to the low bed and a chair, there were small tables and bookcases and wooden stools and rolled-up carpets all around him; this was clearly somebody's storage room for cast-off junk. It faced a long hallway with a doorway halfway down on the left, set in the side of a staircase. Heavy draperies ran all along the right-hand side, and the ornate front door of the house was sometimes visible all the way at the end. There was something familiar about these surroundings, but they were seldom lit well enough for him to figure out just why that was.

He usually just lay in the bed with his eyes closed or half-closed, listening to his own breathing and the sounds of the dark house around him. Sometimes, usually when close to sleep, he thought he saw someone in the hallway before him, or in the doorway of his room, or even right next to his bed. On the dim mornings after such an occurrence, when she came to feed him, he thought to ask the woman not to come near his room in the night, but it never made sense to ask it...the strange figures moving around in the night were either too big or too small to be her, in every case. When *she* moved about the house, she always had her kerosene lantern or a candle, but there was nothing in the room itself to light the night, and each strange, nighttime visitation was similarly unlit. He once managed to ask her who else was in the house with them, and she replied simply that it was just the two of them there, and no one else.

When he eventually managed to sit up in bed for short periods, he was able to use the bedpan by himself with great effort. John didn't care to think about how these needs had been handled while he had been unconscious and recuperating. He was naked beneath the covers, with no clothes in evidence. When he asked the woman—she said her name was Lenore—about his clothes, she replied that she had burned them, as no amount of cleaning would be able get all of that blood out.

The next night, he again heard quiet sobs down the long dark hallway outside the room. Slowly, they grew louder, as if the crier was moving closer while also succumbing to deeper and deeper depths of sadness. This time, there *was* some illumination: a dim light appeared all the way down at the other end of the hall—growing larger as the sobbing person, carrying a small candle, moved closer to the entryway. The candlelight eventually illuminated the front door of the house, the entry with a large circular rug, and the far part of the hallway.

It was at this moment that John realized where he was. This house was Everbridge Manor, the house where he grew up... and he was in the back bedroom, downstairs. This room had once been his own bedroom, but the bed had been higher and in a different part of the room, which is why he didn't recognize it. There was a window in the room, too, bright and visible when he had lived here, but now completely covered by a bookcase. The clutter and the opposing orientation had thoroughly masked the room's distinct familiarity.

A woman came into view at the end of the hallway. The grandfather clock, which he now recalled with perfect clarity as the old clock from which his mischievous sister had once stolen the chains and chimes, years ago, ticked on. Across from the clock, the doorway on the left-hand side of the hallway led down to the basement; John shuddered when he thought about the rotting vegetable smell that often wafted up from there, and how Kitty would sometimes hide in the stairwell and jump out at him as he passed.

The woman down the hall was *not* Lenore; she was a plump, old woman wearing servant's clothes: a long black skirt and a black blouse buttoned all the way to the top. The word *matron* came to John's mind to describe her. She carried a sputtering candle and came to a stop at the foot of the stairs, in the entryway before the closed front door. Her large body spasmed with each of her tremendous sobs.

John was sitting up in the bed, as yet unwilling to test the strength of his legs. He scooted back into the headboard, calling to the woman: "Madam?" He had been speaking so little that the word came out as a clipped croak, startling him further.

A moment later, the matron spoke quietly through her sobs. "How?" she asked, still facing the closed front entrance. "How can you ask this of me?"

The crying woman continued to stare straight ahead. The hallway clock fell silent as she said, "This...this is just evil." She stood there trembling for a few more seconds, clutching her insufficient candle, when suddenly, the front door flew open and smashed against the entryway wall with a tremendous crash. John was so surprised that he knocked the back of his injured head against the wooden headboard, darkening his already dim vision for a few seconds. He had the terrifying thought that he would pass out right then, and that the strange woman would suddenly rush down the hall to his room while he was knocked out, to smother him with his pillow.

The servant woman did not seem to notice the door flying open, nor did she look down the hallway at John. She stared straight ahead, beyond the empty threshold, so transfixed that her sobbing had ceased. Even though the door was now wide open, little additional illumination came from outside; it was either completely clouded over out there, or tonight there was no moon whatsoever. A thick fog snaked into the entry and rolled toward the front stairs. It moved slowly down the hallway.

John somehow knew what was going to happen next before it actually happened. Outside the front door and completely out of his view, a body fell from the roof above and smashed to the ground. The crunch of the impact—all broken bones and broken branches—made the servant woman stumble backwards. And then she screamed. Where moments earlier she had been quiet and timid in her speech and sobs, now her shriek was so piercingly loud that it caused a spike of pain to jab into John's injured head.

Her screech, so jarring in the relative silence of the manor, continued for three full seconds before ending abruptly in a strangled gasp. She coughed, clutched the upper buttons of her severely-buttoned uniform, and dropped her small candle in order to make the clutching into a two-handed job. "Madam?" John rasped. "Madam, are you all right?"

The old servant woman whipped her head to look down the hall at John, her contorted expression one of intense pain. John knew that her face was flushing a deep, scary red, that her wide eyes were darkening with blood, too. And then she fell backwards toward the front stairway, as wooden and straight as a tree felled in the forest. Her body ended up mostly out of sight, her sensible work shoes being the only things visible to John from his vantage down the hallway. Her candle flickered and went out, leaving the entry in near darkness.

When his vision adjusted a few moments later, John could still make out her feet, sticking out in the entry. They did not move, and John knew she was dead. For ten seconds, he just sat in his bed watching for signs of life that he knew would not appear, wondering if he should chance walking out to her on his unstable feet, and otherwise not knowing what to do.

Someone—or some *thing*—yanked the servant woman's body out of view, causing her feet and shoes to disappear suddenly from John's sight. For another moment, the fog swirled and wafted. Then the front door slammed with another incredible bang, which echoed for a long time into the vast silence that followed.

WHEN LENORE CAME into his room the next morning, John was ready for some answers. "Can you tell me what is happening? Is there someone else here? Last night I saw a strange woman by the front door."

She gently unwrapped the large bandage from around his head. "Your head injury looks mostly healed. That's good news, John." She suddenly took his face by both cheeks and turned him toward her, peering into his eyes. John knew he was getting better, because he felt that thrill he sometimes felt when touched unexpectedly by a beautiful woman. And she *was* beautiful, with long dark hair and hazel eyes filled with intellect and concern. "Your eyes are lined back up again," she said with a grin. "When you came, they were each sort of looking off in different directions."

"Different directions? Oh...that's not good." He looked around the room, checking his vision. Things seemed mostly in focus. The room was dark, lit only by Lenore's lamp and two candles, now burning in wall sconces out in the hallway ahead. "Is this Everbridge Manor?"

"So it is," she replied, handing him a cup with some water. "Hold on a minute; I'll bring you some food."

In the dim light, he confirmed that this was indeed the downstairs bedroom of Everbridge Manor, his childhood home. His room was now a strange storage area for old furniture and odds and ends. He sipped the water. There was one window here, he knew from his experience, but using a large, full bookcase to block it was doing nothing to brighten the persistent gloom.

He became aware of a low humming sound, all around, an odd resonance that set his teeth on edge. His hearing was better now, so John knew this sound was not an artifact of his injury. As Lenore returned with a small bowl of warm, sliced carrots, the reverberation intensified slightly. He ate the carrots slowly, noticing immediately that they were the blandest vegetables he had ever eaten. Lenore was lovely, he thought to himself, but she was no cook. He wondered if it would be rude to ask for some salt.

"I'm so pleased that you're gaining your strength back, Raindrop," Lenore said. "Still, you shouldn't try to get out of bed yet...especially in the night. It's not safe for you."

"Not...safe? Why...not safe?" he asked, a piece of dry carrot sticking in his throat. It seemed ridiculous to him that the manor was unsafe somehow, but then he remembered the strange matron in the hallway—and whatever fell outside the front door—and reconsidered. Someone had died last night... probably *two* people, he thought, so perhaps Lenore had a point.

She didn't seem to mind his question. "You could get hurt, moving about in the dark. Your legs won't be very steady, after those injuries to your head. It might be another day or two before you can walk around without falling."

Everything about Everbridge Manor was decidedly odd to John, and he pressed forward trying to find some answers. "Do you hear that vibration sound?"

She straightened the bedsheet and thought about her answer. John remembered at that moment that he had no clothes on under there. Regarding the vibration—not the nudity—Lenore said, "Oh, you should probably ignore that."

"That's a bit difficult, Lenore; it sort of makes my head hurt. What is it? Is there some kind of machine?"

"It's a reminder," she said quietly, looking toward the bedroom door.

"A reminder? Of what?"

She looked him in the eyes and replied, "I know you have many questions, John. But it's a reminder that we must be careful about what we say here in the manor." There came a distinct clank down the hallway on the way to the entry door; it sounded like someone had hit a pipe with a wrench, once, sharply. John looked toward the sound; Lenore ignored it altogether.

John scowled, unnerved by the rumble and that single, intentional, clank. The rumble was a reminder, she had said, but the clank was a reproach. For what? Despite the strange encounter with the matron the night before, he was still not afraid as he peered in the direction of the sound. "Who else is here? This is ridiculous, Lenore! What's going on...and *why* do we need to be careful? Who's listening?"

Lenore smiled ruefully and laughed once. "Well, there you go! That's exactly why we need a reminder."

John looked at her eyes, which seemed familiar to him. He wondered if he had met her before, in a part of his memory that he could not yet reach. John changed his approach, still unable to let the conversation move on without some information. "Do you know how I *got* like this? I don't remember any of it."

"I can't say, love," she replied. "Your horse hauled you across the bridge one day...you were wrapped up in the reins, bleeding and looking like...like you got yourself run over by a wagon. The back of your head was kind of—" She paused and shrugged. "Well...it was cracked open. I think you were in some kind of a fight, but I didn't see anyone else nearby. What's the last thing you remember?"

He considered for a moment and replied, "I was in Junction City, arranging to come here to River's Edge to meet my stepsister, Kitty. I had heard that she was planning to sell our house...*this* house, Everbridge Manor." This recollection made him realize that he was *in* Everbridge Manor and had not yet seen his sister. He sat forward. "Do you know Kitty? Is she letting you stay here?"

Lenore touched her hand softly to his chest, pressing him back down to the bed. "Let's talk about that another time. We can have some tea and a chat in the parlor, maybe tomorrow. There are some clothes around here that will fit you; I'll bring them by. For now, you should rest." And then she left. With her departure, the low rumble subsided.

John had meant to ask her for a candle or a lantern or some matches, to keep on his nightstand in case of inexplicable nighttime visitors, but he had not gotten around to the request. He had to admit, however, that he was still tired. He closed his eyes and thought of some lizards he had once read about, whose eyes moved independently in all directions. He shuddered and moved on to more pleasant thoughts that involved Lenore's gentle hand on his chest, and slept.

Unsettling dreams—battles and bodies—soon replaced those pleasant half-awake musings. Some hours later, John was having a dream where he stood before the matron, looking up at her as she peered nervously out the front door. While he watched her face, the body fell behind him, as inevitable as the heart attack that would follow. The whump in his dream startled him awake.

It was nighttime again. The two candles still burned in the wall sconces in the hall. A dark-haired boy stood in the doorway.

John could not make out the boy's features, as the scant illumination was behind the visitor, leaving his face in blackness. He was about four feet tall, perhaps five years of age. He wore fancy black overalls—streaked here and there with mud—and a white shirt which was torn at the shoulder. The buttons on the shirt were misaligned, the straps of the overalls different lengths...as if someone had dressed him in his Sunday best but was either careless with the result, or unaware that a boy that age will not keep his clothes tidy for long. John could hear what first sounded like the boy's rapid breathing, but it was actually a quiet, dry chuckling. The boy stepped backwards, running his left hand along the wall, ruffling the curtains.

This bizarre scene was the last straw for him. He muttered, "What in blazes is going on here?"

John decided that he would not sit still, as he had done on the previous night when an old woman had succumbed to a heart attack before his very eyes. He felt that he had nothing to fear from a tiny, yet strange, youngster, and he *would* have his answers. "Boy," he called out, "wait right there a moment – I would speak with you." John swung his legs from the bed, planting them and gradually standing up. He steadied himself for a few moments between the nightstand and a nearby desk table. There was far too much furniture in this small room, he thought, but it did come in handy when you were trying to reassert your ability to walk without falling over.

The little boy ignored what John had said, continuing backwards down the hallway beyond the first candle, which illuminated his face and hair. His black bangs were cut in a straight line, though along a slightly skewed angle. He continued to leer and emit his eerie chuckling sound.

John made the doorway and continued following the boy down the dim front hallway. He trailed a hand along the inside wall to steady himself. The wall gave way slightly, as if there was some kind of oily dampness soaking through. He moved past curtains on his right that covered what he knew to be the windows along the porch outside the front door. The open doorway to the basement was on his left, on the wall formed by the long main staircase, leading down to darkness. A volatile kerosene smell pervaded the hallway, becoming more intense as John passed the black basement stairwell. As always, he used caution going past the doorway, lest his sister pop out to startle him as he passed by unawares.

The grandfather clock that John sometimes heard ticking was just on his right, though it was not ticking at the moment. It was currently still and silent as John's eyes were drawn to its stately clock face. Both hands of the clock were nearly straight up, showing one minute to midnight. He remembered this same grandfather clock from his childhood, though it was now in far better shape than it had been some twenty years earlier. Someone had clearly restored it, polishing the wood of the cabinet and replacing the long multiple chain and spring mechanisms that Kitty had removed at some point in order to subdue her dolls or tie bedroom doors closed.

The big hand of the clock covered the last sliver between it and the twelve, and the old device suddenly stuck midnight, startling John, who had his face right up in it.

The child stopped in the large foyer and plucked the other candle from the holder on the wall, held it for a moment with a flickering glee in his dark eyes. The grandfather clock continued its dozen, jarring, midnight declarations.

"Boy," John said again as he moved beyond the clock and the basement doorway. "Take care with that candle."

The boy suddenly threw his candle to the ground, atop the large rug that stood inside the front door. The floor erupted in flames, far faster than John would have expected. There was clearly something flammable already on the rug and floor. The flames spread away from the boy toward the front room of the manor, revealing some letters and eventually a long, fiery word. The "D" and the "R"'s were backwards, as when words are written by a child...as surely they were, for that child stood in front of his work, threw back his head, and laughed. The word "MURDERER" burned the floor, illuminating the whole hallway and the landing up above in red waves.

Lenore stood at the railing on the second floor, staring down, a look of horror on her face and a wadded blanket bunched under one of her arms.

The word MURDERER grew toward the front door, revealing even more flaming letters. The boy cackled madly and scrunched his shoulders up in amusement as his strange preparations came to their—apparently satisfactory—result. John had just one moment to read the full sentence, "SHE IS A MURDERER" before he felt movement behind him and spun back toward the basement doorway. A tall man suddenly came at him from the darkness of the basement, his arms raised above his shoulders. The man surprised John by smashing both of his hands on the sides of John's head, and he felt their resounding crash all the way in his nose and back teeth as his vision dimmed. John staggered and almost fell. The ring in his ears from the blow resonated and throbbed and did not stop.

Inexplicably, the tall man wore a bowler hat and had tremendously long, bushy sideburns. He scowled, revealing an incomplete set of crooked teeth, and he shoved John toward the front door. "You've done it now, Johnny-boy," he growled.

Though John was dazed from the twin blows he had just

suffered, he might have been able to keep his footing if the little boy had not suddenly been kneeling in the hallway, right behind his legs. John stumbled backward over the boy, falling directly onto the flames of the now-engulfed rug. He felt the searing heat of fire on his hands and face for a few agonizing moments before passing mercifully into darkness.

HE AWOKE YET AGAIN in the back bedroom, spluttering and gasping, angry as a trapped bear. This time he came up from a deep dream where someone had stomped on his head and left him incapacitated in a building that was going up in flames around him. In moments, John was on his feet, checking his face, hands, and arms for signs of burns. Thankfully—and also inexplicably—though his skin was tender from the encounter with the fiery rug last night, he had suffered no real burns.

While not literally on fire, John was figuratively burning up. He was hopping mad at the unexplained circumstances at the manor, the inexplicable dangers cropping up in the night. These encounters barely seemed real to him, and he wondered if they were in fact some kind of evil hallucinations...yet the fire and the blows to the head had felt very real – no hallucinations there. He planned to demand answers of the next person he saw, be it Lenore, Kitty, the tall man with the hat and the side-burns, or even that foul, cackling child. He angrily yanked drawers open and looked all around for some clothes, eventually finding a giant, white, button-down shirt that was long enough on him that he could be decent as he charged about on his newfound mission.

Mostly recovered from his original head injury, he walked steadily and with purpose down the hallway, giving a careful look through the open cellar door on his left, braced for some-body to grab him from the darkness. The front door of the manor was standing open, and voices were coming in from outside; he headed that way.

The walls of the front entry were burned; the former rug was a pile of burnt scraps pushed off to the side. Nobody had made any effort to either clean up from the MURDERER debacle the previous night, but even more surprising to John was that nobody had made any attempt to hide it. For some reason, he was starting to suspect that someone was manipulating him—hiding in a dark place he was known to fear, and popping out to assault him, for example...somehow restoring a clock that he had known to have been broken more than a decade earlier. Removing the evidence of the cackling boy's misdeeds seemed like something that might happen in that environment, and he was relieved in a way not to have to deal with that. Instead, there was the spectacle of smeared, burned letters on the ground, which was disturbing on its own.

As he passed into the entryway, he looked left into the empty parlor and up the long, wide front staircase to the railed landing above. His horse, His Majesty, was upstairs in full saddle, visible behind the wooden railing to one side, meticulously licking some nearby wallpaper. Fired up though he was, John stopped dead in his tracks, trying to process the discrepancy of *house* and *horse* at the same time. This jarring inconsistency took an amount of wind from his sails; he surely didn't know what to make of this.

"What in heaven's name is happening here?" he asked. The horse, with no answer in hoof, continued to prospect the walls.

John walked out the front door, toward the voices. When he got to the porch, he saw that it was nearly evening again, with a roiling charcoal sky that threatened rain. The humble Everbridge was ahead down the path, with trees on either side, as he remembered. It had been at least ten years since he had been to the manor. These trees were not as robust as they had been in those younger days; there was, in fact, not a leaf to be seen. There were only thick trunks and empty, brittle branches all around. He looked to the left down at the town of River's Edge, and was taken aback to see that twin pillars of smoke were rising from it; some buildings had apparently burned down in the town recently. He hoped nobody had been hurt.

He was also surprised to see his step-sister Kitty here, just outside the porch of the manor, talking with a tall man in a bowler hat. He had not seen his sister in several years, and those years had not been kind. She was thin and pale and hunched.

She did not light up with pleasure or recognition when she saw John; instead, she betrayed the look of resignation that someone presents when they have to begin an uncomfortable but necessary conversation. Her mouth quietly said, "John, it's good to see you," but her manner said, "You're not going to like what I have to say." She did not seem to notice John's impractical attire.

The tall man standing with her was the one he had encountered in the hallway the previous evening, the one who had smacked John on the head and pushed him over the evil, crouching, little boy into the flames. The man grinned, showing a mouth of uncared-for teeth, and bellowed, "Well, you must be the famous militia-man brother that Kitty's always dronin' on about!" His voice was altogether too loud for someone standing five feet away.

Kitty shushed the tall man, saying, "Keep it down, Rooster! You know they're sleeping!"

John noticed a slight movement beyond Kitty and the blustery man, which turned out to be the same little boy from last night, lying on the ground about fifteen feet away, unsuccessfully pretending to be asleep.

Kitty, her chin pointed toward the ground, said, "John, this is Rooster. He's my...*husband.*" She paused for a moment before saying "husband," making John think that their marriage was either a new, or perhaps somewhat-regrettable, condition.

The bowler hat man leaned nearer, stuck out his hand, and clarified the matter immediately. He continued shouting: "She means 'common law husband,' Johnny. 'Common law,' like *unofficial,* right? Put 'er there, brother!"

John did not accept the offer of a handshake, instead saying, "Sir! What are you playing at? Why did you assault me in the hallway last night?"

The tall man dropped his hand and assumed a less-pleasant demeanor that suited him far more than the blustery politeness he had recently been pretending to. "You don't need to get all high-and-mighty like that, Johnny. I might just have to *pop* you one, settle you right down." He said *pop* with expert emphasis, making John recollect the double-blow to the head he had received not too long ago. John now stood ready for a fight, should one break out unexpectedly.

The strange boy on the ground behind them scrunched his eyes closed but kept peeking out from one or the other of them, something that appeared to amuse him and make his body shake with suppressed laughter. John could not, for the life of him, figure out what kind of play-acting was going on with the child lying there in that way. Kitty moved to get in between John and Rooster. "Now, boys, let's not let this get all heated. We need to agree about the *house.*"

Now that he was on what appeared to be the familiar ground of confrontation, Rooster was unwilling to step back down from it. "I don't think I like your tone," he said to John, pushing Kitty out of the way, and suddenly jacking his right fist directly at John's face.

Though he was just getting over his injuries, John found that he was still able to make his creaky body ready for fisticuffs. He dodged out of the way of the attack, and swung back at Rooster with his own right hook. It was awkward fighting in the long white shirt, but John was determined; he connected with the tall man's jaw, and the two men were quickly immersed in a back-and-forth brawl. John was a former soldier, as well as a trained constable, and he was not going to let this man get the best of him twice. His blows were not strong, but they were accurate, rocking Rooster's head backward multiple times. The little boy, so eerily positioned on the ground just behind where Kitty and Rooster had been standing, sat up on one elbow and watched the fight with intense interest and a sideways grin. Kitty moved away from the fight, off into the yard, and John lost track of her for a moment while trading jabs and elbows with the looming Rooster. Despite Rooster's size advantage—he was almost a foot taller than John—John was landing some sound punches and planned to end this ridiculous fight within the next few moments.

Kitty returned from where she had gone, which had apparently been to the stump where logs were split for firewood. John saw her out of the corner of his eye, but at that moment he was just leaning in for a resounding punch that would have snuffed out Rooster's lights, and he did not notice that his sister was carrying an axe. When he *was* able to register it, it was too late, and he was leaning too far forward with his killer punch to avoid it. Kitty had the axe up and was viciously swinging it down, right in front of John, right at his nose. With this combination of angle and aim, she could *not* miss.

He braced for the crunch of the axe in his face, but then he was suddenly yanked backwards by his flowing white shirt. Before him, the shirt was sheared directly in half by the axe, from collar to groin, and John stumbled backwards into Lenore. Lenore had pulled him back, just in time for him to avoid being killed by his sister.

Rooster, riled but nearly beaten, elbowed Kitty out of anger, and she dropped the axe and resumed the defeated posture she had shown before the fight began. Lenore leaned past John and grabbed the axe from the ground. "Come with me," she said as she pulled John by the arm toward the house. "We need to talk." Shaken from nearly being killed and now standing essentially naked in the front yard, he didn't argue. As Lenore tugged him to the front door, Kitty and Rooster went back to talking with one another as if nothing had happened, and the little boy turned over on the ground, pretending to pull some imaginary covers up to his neck, to settle in for sleep.

Inside, His Majesty was no longer up on the second floor, but a large man was now standing in almost the same place where the horse had been grazing the wallpaper earlier. He was as tall as Rooster, about six and a half feet tall, but was as obese as Rooster was thin. He wore a businessman's clothes, including an unnecessary, paisley ascot. The man was familiar to John, in that he was the same man portrayed in a nearby portrait. The fancy, overdone painting, hung directly at the top of the stairs, showed the fat man wearing an ascot as well, this one yellow, and the same type of too-tight business clothes. John looked at the man, and the portrait, in the short moment when he was pulled through the entryway.

"Who's that?" John asked, pointing up at the fat man, as Lenore whisked him into the parlor.

"Sit down," she replied, plunking him into a nearby, ornate chair. She noticed that he was tugging on the shreds of his ripped nightshirt, trying to cover what the axe had recently exposed, and tossed him a pillow. "Use this. Stop fussing."

Before sitting down opposite him, Lenore drove the axe directly into the wooden floor near the door to the ruined entryway. "All right," she said. "Let's talk."

LENORE SAT in the chair closest to the fireplace, where a small metal tea pot sat heating on a simple grate. "Would you like some tea?" she asked, and before he could refuse, she poured him a cup. She assumed a look of determination and continued. "You surely have questions, Raindrop, and nothing will dissuade you from asking them. So, let's go through it the way I used to do with my students back when I was a teacher. You ask me a question, and when I can answer it, I will raise my hand. If I can't answer it, I will shake my head."

This seemed unnecessarily complicated for a simple information exchange, and John said so. Lenore just shrugged. John needed answers, however, and therefore agreed to her odd terms with an annoyed nod. Behind him, in the dark kitchen, he heard the unexpected sounds of pots and pans being moved angrily about. When he looked back there, little of the illumination from the fire made it to that other room...but he could see a plump servant woman back in the gloom of the kitchen, behind the long wooden-topped counter he remembered from when he was a boy.

The low rumbling sound was also back, unsettling the hairs on the back of John's neck.

The axe in the parlor's doorway cast its long shadow back toward the front entry, away from the fire.

John recognized the woman in the kitchen as the matron from the other night, somehow alive after what looked like a very realistic heart attack. Her quiet crying was the same, yet now she seemed furious as well as sad. Surely, whomever had yanked her out of his sight that night had not miraculously revived her—he remembered having more of a thought that her body had instead been eaten whole by some unseen malevolent force, mercifully out of his sight beyond the foot of the stairway. And yet, here she was. It wasn't a miracle; he knew without any doubt that it was something else entirely. The matron raised a long, iron griddle above her head, and threw it against a kitchen wall with both hands.

Lenore acted as if this spectacle was *not* going on behind

John, and instead handed him his cup of tea. "It does get noisy around here sometimes. Please...enjoy your tea and ask what you must ask. Let's go with, oh...*six* questions, and perhaps a bonus question, before we talk about more pleasant things."

The tea was bitter—and yet somehow *sour* at the same time—and vastly unworthy of having the word *tea* used in its presence. He pursed his lips. He could taste hints of rosemary, but also tree bark...and possibly, dirt.

"Is the tea not to your liking?" Lenore asked with small, knowing smile. With this smile, John was again struck with how familiar she looked to him, but he could not place how he knew her. Lenore was completely ignoring the racket from behind John. "It's my own brew, using the leaves and roots I have available in the garden."

The weepy matron suddenly growled in the kitchen behind him, sweeping plates and ceramic cups onto the floor, where they smashed loudly. "Hopefully one of those isn't the sugar bowl," John said, "because I could really use some for the tea. Do you have sugar?"

Lenore laughed and favored him with a mischievous smile. "Oo, oh! I can answer that one!" She raised her hand, like a schoolchild volunteering to answer a question in class. "The answer is: 'there is no sugar.' Perhaps you can ask Cartwright for sugar when he comes through in a few weeks. He won't bring it, but you can ask. I would literally kill someone, for a few good cubes."

He started to ask, "Kill?" and also "Who is Cartwright?" but stopped himself with both. He wondered how serious she was about allowing only six questions. Instead, he asked, "Who was that big man upstairs?"

Lenore made a sad face, looked him straight in the eyes, and slowly shook her head. John waited for more of an answer, but then she leaned close and said in a whisper, "Remember, class: a head-shake means I can't answer, raising my hand means that I can."

"*Why* can't you answer?" She shook her head again.

With the constant commotion from the kitchen, John kept looking back, trying to discern what could be seen in the gloom. It was awkward struggling to have a forward conversation while someone flew about in a rage just behind his back. The matron was now pulling knives out of a knife-block, angrily whirling around letting the blades embed in whatever was in the way: cabinets, pots, other cutlery.

John thought he already knew the answer to his next question, but the angry servant's bizarre activity, so close to hand, made him ask it out loud. "Do these people, the strange people here, mean us harm?"

And again, Lenore shook her head. John checked the kitchen as the matron started whacking the long blade of a butcher's knife on the countertop, over and over. When he swiveled his head back toward Lenore, he noticed that the axe, previously embedded in the floor near the entry door, was gone.

He wanted to ask about Kitty and what had been going on in the yard, but he wasn't sure Lenore would know the answer; John would ask Kitty directly the next time he saw her, preferably without as much...confrontation. He wondered if Kitty was staying in the manor, in her old room upstairs. Instead of asking about Kitty or her possible room arrangements, however, he asked his next question based on an intuition, "What is in the basement?" Head shake, as the resonating hum became a little louder. The matron continued her disturbing, livid chopping, though there seemed to be nothing in evidence on the wooden counter that needed cutting.

"How much do you know about what is happening here in the manor?" Head shake.

"What's your favorite color?" Head shake. And then Lenore

laughed with genuine amusement as she realized what he had asked, raising her hand quickly and saying, "I'll answer that one. It's *orange*, my love...my favorite color is *orange*! And I suppose *purple* is a close second."

A *clang* resounded from out in the entry area; it was the same distinct sound he had heard when talking with Lenore the previous day. John now thought that it sounded very much like the steel head of an axe being rapped sharply against some kind of glass.

"Well," Lenore said, "Let's talk about something else, shall we?"

John took a second sip of tea, and decided that two was enough.

Lenore lifted up one of her hands and held it in the air for a moment with the fingers touching, as if she was going to snap her fingers. She held John's gaze. The commotion continued in the kitchen, unabated...and then Lenore snapped her fingers right at the same moment that the matron smashed a giant ceramic serving dish to the floor, making a resounding glass-rending racket. When John looked back, there was no one in the kitchen anymore.

John was not deterred by the jarring noise, instead remembering to focus on the lack of information gleaned from the playful information exchange. "Hold on a moment! It's kind of you to serve me tea and offer the promise of answers, Lenore, but you must know that wasn't very satisfying." He motioned his head back toward the kitchen. "And also, a little terrifying."

"There's only so much I can do, John. Would you like some more tea?" She clearly knew he did not.

"Seriously, that was just...*one* answer! And it was about your favorite color!"

She shrugged and tilted her head. "I do appreciate your interest in my favorite things. It's very sweet."

He noticed a black book on the side table near Lenore's

chair, and decided to ask about that instead. Surely, the topic of *books* was not off-limits. He pointed. "Do all schoolteachers like to read books?"

"I can't speak for *all* schoolteachers, but in my experience, educators favor the written word. I, personally, like to read, and I suppose I get a lot of chances to do it. A *lot* of chances. I have bad dreams when I sleep, so reading is useful to pass the long nights." She gestured around, indicating bookshelves that it was too dark to see, but that John knew were there, all around the house. "There are many books at hand, here at Everbridge Manor."

John—who considered himself a man of action, not a man of learning—had never been partial to books. He thought to himself that he would rather wrestle a grizzly bear than pick up one of these musty tomes and somehow try to read it for pleasure.

Lenore said, "I'm sure you would rather wrestle a grizzly bear or something than read one of these books, John, but you might learn something if you looked through them."

John frowned. "Are you a mind-reader, madam, as well as a book-reader?"

In the entry hallway, just beyond the place where the axe had formerly been wedged, a heavy book spilled out of a bookcase. It hit the floor with a sudden crash, disturbing the ashes left over from the burning rug incident of the previous evening. The brown-bound book landed on its spine with its densely-written pages wide open. No one was nearby.

Lenore looked at the book on the floor without remarking upon the inexplicable way it had arrived there. Then, she looked back at John. "Well, the folk in town called me a witch, years ago. Do you think witches can read men's minds?"

"I certainly would not know," John bristled, thinking protectively to himself about how witches were sometimes known to *bewitch* men's mind with spells and potions rather than to *read* them. And maybe they could move objects with their thoughts. Though he had only taken a few sips, he wondered for a moment what was in the tea.

Lenore slowly got up from her chair and walked to the book. She picked it up, closed it, and regarded the brown leather cover. "Oh, *Platonicus*...it's his philosophic works, with commentary by noted scholars, as well as some annotations. I've definitely been struggling through this one lately." She put it back on the shelf. Before she returned, John had a better view of the black book on her table and noticed it was actually the *Good Book*...which he recognized from when he lived in the house before. Again, he had not been an avid reader of it—had never, in fact, opened it—but his Aunt Agnes spoke about it on occasion and he did remember seeing it on a shelf here in the parlor. He thought that *this* book might be a better subject to discuss than old philosophers and disturbing accusations of witchcraft.

"I see you're reading the *Good Book* there...is it one of your favorites, along with the ancient philosophers and the colors orange and purple?"

"If reading a book many, many times qualifies it as a favorite, I suppose it is. I've mostly *stopped* reading it, though, of late."

"Why?"

"It doesn't have the answers I seek. On the plus side, it does have *your* answers in it."

John started saying, "What does that—" but Lenore interrupted. "You know? There was once a two-month period where *all* I did was read the *Good Book* and pray, day and night. I spoke only to my Maker...no one else..." She smiled mischievously and continued, "...much to the chagrin of the other people in the manor at the time, I guess."

He noticed that the copy of the *Good Book* still looked fairly new, for all that supposed use. There was a square, violet-colored envelope tucked in its pages. He was just thinking to himself that a religious nature is a fine quality in a woman, though perhaps three months of solid prayer was overdoing it, when she continued. "On that subject, though, there was also a period, probably two months as well, where all I did was pray to the devil."

John was taken aback. "Madam!" he sputtered. "How could you say that? Why, that *is* witchcraft, pure and simple!" John was no saint, but he did wisely draw the line at attempting to contact Satan.

"Well, it didn't provide me any satisfaction either, if that helps straighten your skirt out, sir. Witchcraft—potions and spells—can't be *all* bad, John...the unguent I used on your injuries, for example, would probably be called witchcraft by the closed-minded townspeople who ran me out of the school. And sometimes, a spell can bring forth a beautiful wonder. I'll show you. Tomorrow."

He wanted to tell her that witchcraft was perilous, but on consideration he thought that such a warning was superfluous here at the manor, almost trivial, in fact. After all, living in this place *at all* seemed fairly dangerous. *He* was no witch, was not courting the devil...yet he had recently watched someone die, fell into a kerosene-fueled fire, and was nearly split in two with an axe. Surely, being a witch or Satanist was no prerequisite for life-threatening danger here.

John worried a little, however, about this "wonder" that Lenore was hinting at. He decided to change the subject. "Well, I'm feeling good enough that I should get on with something productive. I believe I had business in town, business with my sister. I should get myself cleaned up, too." He indicated his ripped white nightshirt. "And could I trouble you for those clothes you were talking about?"

"Of course!" she said. She opened a drawer in the table beneath the *Good Book* and withdrew a long, orange strip of cloth. It was the waist-tie from a robe or a dressing gown. "This should do, to start, with more tomorrow morning. And you can have a bath in the stream...do you remember the spot for that?"

He did indeed remember the small inlet of the stream, surrounded by strategically-planted trees, where he and his family had washed themselves, back in the days when he lived at the manor. He nodded.

A long envelope whisked into view, sliding along the floor from the dark, empty entry hall, into the space between John and Lenore. They both stared at it, as if it was a giant, unwelcome, paper insect.

Lenore sighed, looking down at the sudden envelope in the room. "Don't worry about remembering your business in town, John. There will be constant reminders."

John stared at the envelope, not moving to touch it. It had a wax seal on it that he recognized as the seal of Junction City. Someone had written, "Official Business" below the seal, in a careful script. "Are we to ignore that this house seems..." He paused, and continued, "...well, *haunted*, Lenore? There's nothing *normal* about books hopping from shelves by themselves, or letters flinging themselves across the floor."

She slowly shook her head. "That's your bonus question, Sunshine. I can't answer it."

John stood, tied the robe-tie around his waist, and bent to pick up the envelope. He turned it over to the front. It had his name written on it, also in a deliberate, official hand. He turned it over to the back again, and reached a finger to open it.

Lenore put up her hand. "It's a might chilly in the parlor here, John...perhaps you could throw that wretched envelope on the fire and see if it warms us any."

He frowned. "Why would I do that? It's addressed to *me*... official business from Junction City."

"That's what it looks like, sure...but it is a lie. A distraction. Nothing good will come from reading it."

"Why should I believe you? You've *barely* been helpful, Lenore, despite us talking here over tea for half an hour!"

"Would you believe that we've talked for that long, and yet I haven't lied to you once? It's a challenge, believe me...you ask a lot of tricky questions." She shrugged. "And rightly so, to be fair."

He tapped the envelope on his hand, looking at the fire but not yet opening what he held.

Lenore pulled the square, violet envelope from the *Good Book* and leaned close to John. She spoke quietly, as a tink-tink-tink sound came from the vibrating front hallway. It wasn't the same sharp warning clank they had heard before, but it was a close cousin. "You don't want *that* envelope, my love...but you *do* want *this* one." He could see a wax seal on the back with an ornate letter "L".

John considered the offer, but did not move toward any decision. She continued, slightly louder, as if in performance. "After all that delicious, unsweetened tea, you probably need to use the outhouse, right, John? You'll remember it from your previous time here–it's in the same place, off to the right as you leave the front porch." John nodded; he knew where it was. "Take a lantern, and you can attend to your *business*"—she lifted her violet envelope slightly—"before turning in for the night. I'll see you in the morning. Around noon, I'll cast my spell. You won't want to miss it."

John thought about how she had just saved him from getting chopped in two by his own sister. He also remembered being pushed into a fire as he fell unconscious, and yet waking up with few burns; he was fairly sure that Lenore had seen to that outcome as well. He had to admit that he was extremely intrigued about the violet envelope. John made a sudden decision to trust her, for now. It was entirely possible that she *hadn't* lied to him, but then, some of what she had said, if so, was truly difficult to believe. He took the violet envelope, tucked it into the waist of his shirt/robe, and tossed the "official business" envelope on the fire.

Lenore smiled and pretended to warm her hands. "You've got to start somewhere."

JOHN WAS glad to have a functional lantern as he walked out the front door of the manor; he planned to leave it on, roughly, forever. The night had fallen outside, though the day had been so dark that there was little difference. It was raining slightly, which emphasized the impractical attire he was wearing. Kitty, Rooster, and the eerie faux-sleeping child were nowhere to be seen. He headed around to the right, moving past the long porch, toward the old, reliable outhouse. From his youth, he remembered the carved half-moon in the creaky door, and inside, a solid seating plank with a foul hole.

He noted two strange things as he approached the outhouse, though at this point he was starting to take them in stride. First, there was a hunched old woman standing on the porch near the house. She wore a heavy black shawl, pulled up over her white hair, and she looked like she was almost a century old. It was not Lenore, not the matron, not Kitty. It was yet another woman entirely, this one with long, straight white hair down to her waist. Those white locks bracketed her wrinkled face in two vertical strokes and one horizontal, like the top of a doorway. Her mouth was closed in a tight, severe line. Her eyes were dark, almost black. She said nothing as he passed.

For a moment, John envied her that protective shawl as he felt the chill of the night's rain and low fog. He had no hat to tip as he said, "Evenin', ma'am," but then again, he had no pants, for that matter.

Next, he saw a strange, irregular pillar of blue light way off in the brittle trees, far beyond the outhouse, behind the manor.

It was too far away for him to make out what it was, but it rose all the way to the clouds in the roiling sky, connecting the ground and the heavens in a vibrating glow. John nodded. "Not something you see every day," he said quietly to himself.

As he got to the outhouse, he noticed that the old woman had come off the porch and was now walking slowly, so slowly, toward him. Her frail feet and small strides barely helped her cover much ground at all. Even so, he wasn't sure he could complete his business before she crossed the distance, but he decided to give it a try.

He quickly pulled open the outhouse door, which emitted a long, loud creak that was exactly as it had always been. The sound brought back memories of many trips out here. When he was a boy, he got quite good at visiting these facilities in the deepest part of the night without being scared at all, and he tried to remember that skill for this visit. He swung the lantern in to check for occupants—Kitty would sometimes tuck herself around behind the door and startle him after the door closed— but there was nobody inside. He entered, pressed the hook latch into its eye-bolt, and moved to get down to his biological business. He almost forgot the violet envelope as he lifted the nightshirt, and he bobbled it; it started to tumble toward the dark, foul-smelling hole, but he caught it just in time. He sat down over the hole. It felt good to perform all of these menial bodily functions in the normal way; he didn't realize how awkward and unpleasant the bedpan had been.

He slid his finger into Lenore's "L" envelope and ripped the top open. Suddenly, a bang rang out, as somebody slammed the outhouse from the outside. He remembered the strange old woman shuffling deliberately toward the outhouse, but doubted that *she* could have mustered the force needed for that blow; in fact, it seemed like it came from all four sides at once.

"Almost done!" he called out, as he pulled a piece of perfumed, violet paper from the envelope. It had several lines written on it, in a beautiful, ornate, feminine script. He read them quickly, as more blows rained on all of the sides of the outhouse.

"No sugar. Nothing sweet whatsoever."
"A beast."
"They will kill us."
"They will kill us."
"Kerosene in glass jars, and candles. Lots of kerosene."
"Everything."
"Orange, for the sunrise. Purple, for the sunset."
"Bonus: Yes, Ignore it. Protect yourself."

After the last line was a lovely, cursive letter "L".

He read all the lines again, mentally tracking them back to all of the questions to which they were the miraculous answers. It was a crazy, impossible magic trick. And processing the answers was hard, with that horrific pounding on the walls – he thought the outhouse would be knocked on its side with the level of force being used.

Then he dropped the violet paper and envelope into the hole. As he closed his shirt and wrapped the orange tie around his waist, a piece of paper slapped over the half-moon cutout on the outside of the outhouse door and stuck there, fluttering as if in a strong breeze. John pushed the door open and found the old woman right there in the doorway, her gray, aged face brightly illuminated in the lantern he was holding up. She did not speak. John registered for a moment that the scary old woman looked like the Innkeeper from River's Edge – or perhaps like that woman's mother or grandmother. She was just *so* old, and her eyes were *so* black, it was a terror to regard them.

The rain was really starting to come down now. The outhouse door banged shut, revealing that the paper covering the cutout was the "official business" envelope he had just burned in the fire. John left the now-wet envelope there, jittering against the half-moon even though there was no wind in evidence to hold it up there, and he pushed roughly past the old woman. She weighed so little that he was able to move her aside easily—but he could feel how bony she was from just their brief contact.

John ran through the rain back to the manor. He noticed his horse, His Majesty, saddled up and standing stoically on the Everbridge, and wondered if he should just walk over to his mount and ride away. This made a great deal of sense, given the dangerous things happening all around here, but without a memory of how he came to this place, he wasn't entirely sure where he would go. There was also the matter of clothing: a ripped nightshirt and a robe tie didn't really seem like the right things to be wearing when considering a ride. Lastly, John admitted to himself that he was intrigued by what he had just read on Lenore's note, and was curious about the grand "wonder" Lenore was talking about, somehow planned for the next day. When he looked back toward the outhouse, the old woman had turned and was again walking toward him.

He forgot about the horse and decided to move indoors quickly. He made it through the front doorway, closed it behind him, and turned the key that was—thankfully!—in the lock, securing it. The idea of going down the hall to his old bedroom —filled with claustrophobic clutter and already the scene of several disturbing encounters since his time back at the manor —did not appeal to him. Instead, he went back to the parlor, hoping to talk more with Lenore, though for some reason he felt it would be a bad idea to bring up her startling, violet answers out loud.

She was indeed still in the parlor, now sleeping fitfully in the chair next to the fire. What she had said about bad dreams was clearly true, for she jerked and spasmed as if in the throes of the worst kind of nightmare, her eyes closed and moving wildly beneath their lids. John watched her for a minute or so, unsure of what to do, and all the while she continued to fret and sway while some imagined terror reigned in her sleep.

John sat down on the floor before her chair, slowly taking one of her hands in his. She squeezed it repeatedly, still sleeping...but over time, her alarming shudders diminished slightly. She didn't *stop* having her nightmare, but it seemed less terrifying somehow. Eventually, John, too, fell into a restless sleep.

JOHN AWOKE ALONE on the parlor floor in the morning. Lenore was not in the nearby chair, nor in evidence at all. In the doorway leading to the entry, he found a tidy wicker basket with a lump of handmade soap, a rolled-up brown towel, a giant beige shirt, and a pair of large canvas pants. Some fancy material had been hand-woven into a long, thin, rope-tie, which he assumed was to be used to keep the massive pants from falling down. He noted that the fabric of the rope tie looked very much like the elaborate paisley ascot that the bejowled man wore in the portrait atop the stairs.

While some things in the manor "appeared" by some type of frightful magic, John suspected that this simple basket had just been set there for his use, by Lenore. She was not in the kitchen, which instead hosted strewn cookware and shards of ceramic cups, plates, and bowls. Several long knives stuck out of the upper cabinet doors. While he was in there, he drew a small measure of water from the kitchen pump and drank it, considering as he did how strange it was that he wasn't particularly hungry or thirsty, and had not been for a while, despite having only had a few sips of miserable tea the night before. Besides the memorably bad tea, he could not remember the last time he drank or ate.

Lenore wasn't in the entry, with its scuffed black ashes and haunted bookshelves. She was not in the hallway that lead to his back bedroom, with the spongy walls and the oily smell that was most intense atop the basement stairs. He didn't check the back bedroom itself, nor the basement, which chilled him from an ancient place of childhood fears.

He assumed that Lenore was elsewhere in the house or grounds, so he decided to use her supplies to get cleaned up in the stream. It had surely been weeks since he had arrived at the manor, and if he had been bathed at all during that time, it was while he was unconscious, and it was done by Lenore herself. When thinking about how much this woman had attended to his personal needs during his recuperation, John felt a little awkward; she was *very* familiar. He had to admit that there was part of him—that part that was not mortified at these unrequested intimacies—that liked them.

The gray skies that had been in evidence every time John had gone outside had not relented. Instead, the clouds were so dark and thick that it was hard to tell that it was daytime, and fog still rolled along the grounds. He made his way to the section of the stream where he and his family once bathed, screened from the nearby Everbridge with careful trees. The trees were nothing like they were back then; there was not a single leaf to be seen. But the straggly branches still blocked most of the view, and he felt that the fog and generally-inhospitable weather would keep passersby to a minimum. He stripped off his billowy, ripped white shirt, took up Lenore's handmade soap, and entered the chilly water.

It was indeed a cold bath, here in the old stream, but it still felt very good. His head was no longer fuzzy from a fractured skull, and he felt like he had gotten his strength back after being out of commission for what was probably two or three weeks. The water was up to the middle of his thigh, with a slight current pulling gently downstream, toward town. The soap did the job, but it was harsh; when it got in his eyes one time, he felt like it would burn away his eyesight. He had just soaped up his hair and face, closing his eyes tightly to avoid becoming permanently blinded, when he heard someone coming his way.

He swiped the soap a bit and looked through squinty eyes to see Lenore heading down the bank to the bathing spot. She wore a yellow robe and carried a wicker basket that was exactly the same as *his* basket, currently on the shore right next to all of his clothes. She had some of her own clothes under one arm.

"Good morning, John," she called cheerily as she approached the edge of the water. He had nothing to cover his body with, nothing in his hands except for the soap, in fact, and he felt that it would be foolish to use that little lump as some kind of tiny modesty shield. After all, *she* was the one who had approached this bathing spot, surely knowing full well that John would be here and would be unclothed. This was no accident; her amused expression told him so.

John used one hand to cover his privates, ineffectively, and said, "Madam, as you can see, I'm bathing here. Some privacy would be welcome."

She ignored this and smiled, saying, "You're not the only one who's a little dirty, John."

Lenore set her basket and dry clothes down on the bank next to John's while asking, "How is the water? Is it chilly this morning?" And then, without a bit of hesitation, she removed her robe. Just like that, not twenty seconds after "Good morning," she was suddenly, completely naked. If she had meant to shock and tease John, her commitment to the prank was absolute. She picked up her own slab of soap, and stepped into the stream to a position right next to the stunned John.

Lenore cupped cold water from the thigh-high stream and let it run down her front, over and over. "I wish you would stop calling me, 'Madam,' John. It makes me feel my age."

She was still quite a young woman in John's estimation; he had a very good view from this near vantage, he couldn't help but notice that she appeared no more than 30 years old. She began to lather her body, seeming to pay him little attention. "And how old would that be?" John asked, before he could help himself. His brain was not completely engaged.

"John! How *forward* of you! You know it's inappropriate to ask a woman her age, don't you?"

He knew she *had* to be joking. She was, after all, standing there wearing only what she was born wearing, baiting him by splashing water up over her breasts. "*Forward*?" John said. "It may be, but for some reason I feel that it's not the *most* shocking thing to occur in the last minute or so." He considered that for a moment and then added, "And of course I meant no offence, my lady."

"Oh, none taken, Sunshine," she replied. "I assure you, if I took offence that easily, I should surely have pitched myself from the gables on the first gray day of winter." She smiled and lazily continued her bathing, reveling in his nearby awkwardness, his feeble hand shielding his parts. John was amazed at how comfortable *she* was, so close to him, and so...*everything*. It seemed that modesty had no place here in the bathing hole at Everbridge Manor this morning, and he made the same kind of bold decision he had made in tossing the Junction City envelope into the fire the previous evening. It took some courage, but when he did it, he was actually surprised at how easy it was. After one deep breath, he stood up straight, cast his own shyness aside, and went back to his ablutions. It was either that, or continue to stand there with one hand held awkwardly over his crotch, while she undertook no such efforts, soaping and splashing and smiling just three feet away.

Lenore watched him slyly as he got back down to the business of washing, and he, in turn, watched her. She rubbed her beautiful, large breasts with soap, meticulously lathering them, and also her long hair, and her arms, and her legs, and her lovely neck, and John needed to *stop*…just *stop* watching, it was insensitive, and yet *she* was the one who came out here, knowing that *he* was here, too, and he could hardly manage to avert his eyes. It was unnerving and exciting and altogether pleasant, and John was pretty sure that she was feeling the same way. They could both tell that John was fully recovered from his injuries.

He washed the soap from his own hair, which was growing quite long, and Lenore said, "If you wish, I can trim your hair for you. I'm very skilled; I'm sure you'll like my work."

"Is there some kind of 'witch spell' for that?"

She laughed, and John thought to himself that he was starting to enjoy the sound. "Perhaps there is, but I just use scissors."

At the risk of spoiling an otherwise entirely agreeable moment of unexpected, shared bathing, John could not let their strange circumstances go unremarked. There had been too many unexplained occurrences in the past few days. "What of the strange events in the manor? I still have many questions. What would happen if we talked about that, out here?"

She motioned to the straggly trees that surrounded the bathing hole. Her body was so lovely to behold, John thought, and she was so relaxed standing next to him, it was intoxicating. John had been with women in his time, but none had been as striking and mysterious and beautiful as Lenore, as she stood before him now. "These trees would probably attack us."

John frowned and waited for her to say, "Just kidding," but she did not. He hadn't expected *that* answer—retaliatory trees, of all things!—though on further thought he wasn't really sure what answer he *had* expected, besides the now-familiar "I can't answer that." Of course, she might also choose the option of slipping him a piece of paper on which the answers to his questions had been written, seemingly before any questions had been either imagined or spoken. "Lenore, didn't you say you would try to be truthful, when you actually answer my questions?"

"All right then," she laughed. "These trees would probably burst into flames and *then* attack us."

John shook his head. That was no better...worse, in fact. He decided to let the subject drop. He waded to the shore, used his brown towel to dry himself, and put on the clothes that Lenore had provided for him. "Please don't run off, John," she said, blithely using her soap on parts of her body that John was sure she had already washed. "You have to help me with my weather spell this morning, remember?"

"Yes, I remember, though I'm not sure how much patience I'll have for witchery, if I'm to speak honestly myself. I'll leave you to finish your bath." If he was being really truthful, he would have said that he would like to *stay* while she finished her bath, but he was a gentleman, even after being so teasingly provoked.

"As you wish, my love. I'll be done in a moment."

JOHN WALKED UP to the manor and took up a seat at the outside table, on the long front porch. While he waited for Lenore to come up, too, he thought about his present situation. There were so many disturbing aspects of the last few days, primarily the strange, angry people all around who were there one second and gone the next. It was madness, to be sure, whether they were real or imagined. He did wonder if that was all an insane artifact of his head injury, but living the rest of his life with terrifying hallucinations was a truly an unpleasant prospect to consider. He set that aside and thought instead about his total lack of recollection of what he had been doing before he arrived here. And again, his head injury had been so severe, he believed, that it had violently erased an indefinite period from his memory.

This was not the first time John had experienced a memory gap. He had little recollection of any time *before* he lived with Kitty and his Aunt at the manor, though he knew he was at least five years old when he began living there. But a dim memory of childhood events wasn't unusual for most people; being unable to remember what happened to him, as a grown man, that had led to a terrible injury just a month ago, was much more troubling.

How long was the gap? The last thing John could remember was hearing about his step-sister from a colleague who had returned to Junction City from some work over in River's Edge. This could have been four weeks ago, or maybe eight; it was hard to tell what time of year it was when the weather was so universally gray.

John's colleague, Rolf, was an older investigator who sometimes worked cases with him in bustling Junction City, and the older man had lived in River's Edge during some of the time that John and Kitty were there growing up. Kitty and John had the same father, but different mothers, making them step-brother and step-sister, and all of their parents were deceased. Rolf had known the children during the early years when they lived at Everbridge Manor with their prim, quiet Aunt Agnes, before the pair had each left River's Edge for other pursuits. John had been a serious young man, and he went to join the militia at the age of eighteen; Kitty had always been flighty and unreliable, and she just left around that same time, occasionally making her presence known here or there, but often letting years pass without any contact at all. It should have been worrisome to lose track of her, charging off as she did for long periods of time unannounced, only to return with no suitable explanation days or weeks later...but it wasn't. Finding out that Kitty had run off was a continuous occurrence since she had been around ten years old.

Rolf, the old investigator, was surprised and delighted to see Kitty in River's Edge, surely having decided a long time before that her wild ways would bring her to a bad end. When he greeted her, he learned of her ongoing plans to sell Everbridge Manor. Kitty was the sole owner of the property and could sell it for money if she so wished, had in fact often talked about liquidating it, over and over while they were teens...saying she planned to use the money for this scheme or that. To call her schemes *ill-considered*, John thought, was to incorrectly imply that there had been consideration. One time she was going to buy a horse ranch. Another time, perhaps wishing for the same guidance herself, she mused about creating a home or school to guide anxious or fearful young people away from their troubles. Yet another time, she wanted to build a cottage in the woods near Four Corners, leaving everything and everyone behind. John didn't trust her ability to hang onto the proceeds after she had them. Beyond the thought that she would use the money unwisely, John had been keen to avoid having his childhood home sold at all, if that could be prevented. Spending the last few, strange weeks here, however, was starting to change his mind about that.

He had been making arrangements to head to River's Edge to talk her out of it, when...well, when the next thing he remembered was being half-dead atop His Majesty, enduring the jagged, vice-like pain all around his head, barely being able to see or hear Lenore as she spoke to him on the manor path. What had happened in between? John couldn't say.

Behind him, the front door of the manor was slowly opened from inside by a skinny man wearing overalls and a workman's cap. The door creaked ominously as it swung inward, and the smell of oil or kerosene wafted to the porch. John turned to look back just as the man retreated into the shadows of the entryway. John popped to his feet and rushed that way, no longer content to let these troubling people jump out at him, chase him into the outhouse with his tail and a violet envelope between his legs, or trip him into impromptu blazes. When he stepped into the entry, however, there was nobody there. He peered left down the long corridor to the back bedroom and thought to himself that he would be happy never to go down that hallway again. A single candle burned on the wall, near the ticking grandfather clock, across from the basement stairwell. Way down in the cluttered room at the end, John thought he saw a person sitting in the low bed. The shape was *wrong* somehow, but it was too dark to tell who or what it was. If it had been a person, it was someone with oversized, black, angular eyes, and a giant, almost circular, head.

John's gaze was drawn to the right to some movement in the parlor. There, a thin woman in a dusky, ruffled dress sat in Lenore's chair, slowly beckoning to him.

Incredibly, it was yet a *different* woman...not Lenore, nor the matron, nor the old lady who looked like the town Innkeeper. John felt like he needed a ledger to keep track of all of the faces he was seeing around these dark manor rooms...and so many of them women. *This* woman was in her late-thirties, with long, braided black hair streaked here and there with grey. Her clothes were frayed in some places, visibly repaired in others. Unlike the distraught matron or the slack, wrinkled face of the Innkeeper, this person wore a calm expression. She seemed vaguely familiar to John, as if she was somebody he knew when he was very, very young, perhaps before he even came here to live with Kitty and Aunt Agnes. Despite the familiarity, he had absolutely no intention of taking her up on the beckoning motion she was performing.

Quietly, the woman said, "Come along, John."

Lenore was coming up from the bathing hole and called faintly from outside. "John?"

He looked left, down the hallway again, and now the strange shape that had been in the bed was in the bedroom doorway. It filled *most* of the doorway, in fact, taller than a tall man. It was not human...John was sure of that now. It was completely still; he had not seen how it moved from the bed to the door. It wore a crummy straw hat and a billowy white shirt like the one he had been wearing himself just a short while earlier. The candle on the wall fizzled and burned out, but after the moment of adjustment to the darkness, John could still see whatever that was—the thing with the bag-like, round head and murky eyes—down there in the doorway, dead still.

As Lenore called, "John?" again, closer now, he backed slowly out the front door, not taking his eyes off the dark hallway. As Lenore approached on the path, John stepped to the porch. He looked over at her as she moved to take a seat at the porch table. Then, fearing that the wretched face would be squashed right in the gap in the front door when he looked back that way, he was thankful that there was nothing there at the door or visible down the hall, or if there was, it was too dark to see it.

John shuddered, pulling the front door closed. These visions—what he was starting to think of as *evil spirits*—were no longer just scary people who wished to hurt him, they had progressed to being actual monsters. Not good. He decided that if he saw Kitty again, he would agree outright if she wanted to sell the manor. Everbridge Manor had a squatter—an accused witch who was also a self-admitted, part-time devil-worshipper —and that squatter acted like she owned the place. Let her have it, he thought. Let her have it for *free*, in fact. But beyond the muddy issue of ownership, Everbridge Manor also had a major *pest* problem, which John knew would not be solved by simply backing out some door and closing it behind.

———————— ❧ ————————

LENORE SAT at the porch table wearing a burgundy dress and a furrowed brow, facing out toward the front path and the bridge while the gloomy grey skies churned above them. John was still unsettled from the two spirits he had just seen inside the house, and he looked mistrustfully up to where Lenore was gazing. It looked to him as if there were layers and layers of dark clouds all around, stacked atop each other lest some type of daylight accidentally peek through.

"Sometimes the weather around here feels like having the covers pulled up over my head," Lenore said sadly. Her mood was no longer flirty, as it had been at the bathing hole; she squinted her eyes slightly, as if against tears. John wondered what had happened to bring on this change in mood.

He thought about what would happen should someone act out the "covers" metaphor Lenore was using; surely, something ugly would mill around beyond the flimsy sheets. There would be no comfort, to be sure, from that age-old, childish gesture of using a piece of bedding to block sight in both directions. "Pulling the sheets up over one's head seems like an unwise idea, here at Everbridge Manor," he said, and she nodded.

They sat there in silence for a bit, and John could feel her attitude and demeanor changing by the second, as if darkened by the troubled skies above. "Are you all right, Lenore?" he asked.

"Yes...yes," she replied, touching a finger to the corner of one of her hazel eyes. "I usually don't let things bother me, but I'll admit that I'm not always successful."

The low hum rose from inside the manor, as if a large group of katydids started working their wings at once, and continually. It was the same buzz that he had heard previously, when he and Lenore set to conversation. "I believe it's time for our wonder to commence, John." She got up and opened the front door to the manor, raising the volume on the hum considerably. She gathered a two-foot stack of heavy books from a shelf just inside, and propped the front door completely open.

"Why did you do that?" John asked.

"You'll see," she said. When she sat back down, she had some tears on her cheeks. "You'll have to help me with this spell, John, okay?" He had planned to hold his arms crossed in front of him, to ward off participation in any cursed form of deviltry, but her tears disarmed him a bit. The grandfather clock inside the house began to "bong," marking the twelve o'clock hour. "Don't worry, your participation won't cause the Junction City Chamber of Commerce to kick you out of town for practicing witchcraft, if that's what you're thinking."

She placed her right hand on the table, palm up. When she said, "The spell works best if you're holding my hand," her voice broke slightly.

He frowned, not moving to take her hand.

"It's okay, John," she said, with the weakest of smiles. "It's just my hand, not my hand in marriage."

He took her hand as the clock struck its twelfth gong, and she squeezed him tightly, at the same time as her eyes. The act of pressing her eyes shut caused more tears to get wrung out, and they ran in two trails down her face as the hum from the house turned into a rumble. John wondered where the flirtatiously composed woman from the pond had gone. The quivering katydid sound had been replaced by something more akin to the clatter of moving wagons. A wind kicked up from nowhere in particular. Had the trees around here ever managed any leaves that fell to the ground, John thought, those leaves would have been spinning.

John looked up into the black sky, where the clouds were starting to swirl. It was some kind of amazing, localized tornado, just above the manor, encompassing every bit of sky that he could see, in all directions. And then the wagon-train rumble from the house turned into a roar, the sound of standing beneath a tremendous waterfall, accompanied by the ground actually shaking, as if in a world-quake.

Suddenly, there came the devastating, ringing crash of thick glass being smashed—exploded, somehow—from inside the manor, followed by a huge rush of oily air straight out the front door. Breathing it almost burned the inside of John's nose. If the front door had been closed, instead of propped open with books as it currently was, it would surely have been blown from its hinges. It was as if some massive bellows had been triggered inside, blasting the intense smell of kerosene across John and Lenore on the porch, probably disturbing the bare branches of trees all the way on the other side of the river. John looked back toward the house, feeling that any nearby candle that had not been blown out by that blast of air would have caused an explosion, probably killing them both. He continued to grip Lenore's hand, each of them now squeezing the other firmly.

When John looked back out toward the manor grounds, the sky there was completely clear. He could almost *feel* his pupils constricting with the sudden change in brightness. It was blindingly blue, all around, not a cloud in sight, and he could feel the warmth of a brilliant sun on his face and arms.

"Sunshine!" he shouted, and Lenore laughed quietly, opening her eyes and turning her face up to the sky, where her tears sparkled in the newfound light. The sun was *there*, resoundingly bright and orange, for goodness sake! And the blue sky! John could hardly believe it. The rumble and ground-shaking and echoing sounds of smashed glass had all subsided, though the thick smell of kerosene was still all around.

John had enjoyed days of blue-sky weather back in Junction City, perfect days, hundreds and hundreds and hundreds of them...probably as recently as a month ago, in fact, but he had carelessly overlooked them. What a sin that had been! If it was a miracle *right now*, and John knew it was, it had been the exact same miracle every other time he had waltzed through a beautiful, sunny day without taking any real notice of it. He *knew* it had been a mistake—an affront, really—to take the amazing blue of the sky—the luscious warmth of the sun!—for granted, as he had done so many times before.

Lenore was looking all around, soaking in the splendor as John was, while her chin quivered with emotion.

"What has happened?" John asked quietly, as the sky gained the hints of majestic purple that it sometimes showed during the most beautiful sunsets. He also wanted to ask her why she hadn't cast this spell earlier; the effect was exquisite. Witchcraft or not, he wanted it to last forever. The grounds of Everbridge Manor were so bright and clear, he could feel his whole body, his heart, soaking up the sun's heat.

"The vessel of beauty has broken."

And next there came a sudden crash of thunder, one blinding white flash of lightning that encompassed the whole sky, and the black clouds were back again. Lenore closed her eyes, as her body started to rock with sobs. John took her hand into both of his, almost feeling like he could cry himself. He said, "No," in the quietest voice, before he could stop himself. All told, the sky had been clear for perhaps thirty seconds, maybe as much as a minute, but when he looked up now, it was as if all that had never happened.

"I...I...can't," Lenore managed to say, in between unsteady gasps. "I'm sorry. I can't...do it anymore."

This was the first time John had seen her discomposed, despite averted ax-murders, crashing cutlery, mysterious missives. John sputtered, "What...it?" as Lenore pulled her hand from his and ran into the house, still crying.

John looked for another moment at the perplexing gray sky all around, but then followed Lenore inside the manor. She ran up the wide front staircase to the second floor, heading toward the smaller stairway that lead to the high roof of the manor. John ascended the stairs and noticed that someone had driven the ever-present Everbridge Manor axe into the face of the fat man in the portrait on the second-floor landing. The axe had actually been driven through an official-looking envelope with the Junction City seal, and *then* into the skewed painting. The envelope was slick with an oily liquid that was coming from the hole. John ducked under the protruding axe handle as he hurried up the next set of steps after Lenore.

The rooftop door opened outward to a small, flat, roughly shingled area, which gave to a steep incline ahead, with a few peaks on either side. Except for the flat part just outside the doorway, the whole roof was made up of precarious slopes and precipitous angles, formed from various gables. When John came out of the rooftop doorway to the flat area, he saw Lenore out where the steep downward angle jutted over the front of the house. She was walking right on the edge, sometimes looking down, sometimes not. The front garden was thirty feet below.

Inexplicably, John's horse was also up here on the roof, serenely standing on one of the nearby inclines, hind quarters elevated slightly above its head. The animal was calm, as if a high, canted roof was the very place that every horse needed to be. All in all, John thought, a saddled horse on the roof was the easiest thing to believe, of all the things he had witnessed in the last five minutes. Lenore had her face in her hands, walking one way and then the other, hardly looking at her feet, as John slowly approached.

"Lenore," he said, holding out one hand as if to steady her over the distance. "Please step away from the edge." With a single step—or misstep—she would be gone.

A few feet ahead of Lenore, a child's hand slowly rose up from the other side of the ledge. John could not see the body to which it was attached, but he had an idea what it would look like. The strange, evil boy, the one from that night in the fiery hallway, was going to pull Lenore over the edge as she passed by. Lenore did not look down; she was, in fact, currently proceeding along the dangerous ledge with both of her eyes closed. It didn't occur to John to wonder how a boy got right there, how he was possibly wedged or attached or hanging or floating such that he himself didn't fall; his only thought was to protect Lenore.

John rushed the entire remaining distance between the entry door and the edge in five long steps, intending to knock the boy's greedy claw away from Lenore's leg before he could achieve his fiendish desire. The roof's declination, however, was particularly steep, and John's speed was far faster than he intended as he covered the gap. As he reached down toward the grasping hand, the boy's real plan became clear: that hand whipped up and grabbed John by the hair and used the man's momentum to pull him all the way over into the void.

John noticed three things as the world flipped upside down, giving him frantic glimpses of canted horse, shingled inclines, chimney, black sky, open air, and finally the brittle garden below. First, the boy's grasping arm was now blackened and burnt, as was the boy's whole body. This was now a charred, flaking, black and red *thing* perched on an outcropping. It may have had the shape of a child, but this miserable, smoldering mass of flesh was no longer recognizable as one. Second, the garden plot below was tremendously far away; John would surely cover the entire distance to it in just a tiny instant of time, but those three stories would easily be enough to end him forever. Lastly, John learned how agonizing it was to have one's whole leg roughly bear a grown man's entire weight and rotational speed over a steep ledge, all in one moment. His fall was arrested by just a few precious tendons and muscles and bones, all of which wrenched painfully as Lenore managed to snag his left foot when he passed her. She had somehow braced herself to catch his full weight, and in doing so was yanked flat, her chin smashing on the ledge, with both of her arms over the side and her whole body prone on the precipitous roof. John smashed against the side of the manor, rattling his elbows and shoulders. Miraculously, Lenore kept both of them from tumbling all the way to the ground, and now the burned boy was nowhere to be seen.

"Hold still, Raindrop," she said quietly, through her clenched teeth. A trickle of blood appeared on the side of her mouth where her teeth or jaw had impacted the side of the roof. "I can try to pull you up."

"Um...okay, yes," he said shakily. By lifting his head straight up on his neck, he could see the ground clearly. "Try not to...to drop me."

"If I do, you can be sure I'll come right after you."

They hung there for a few seconds, catching their breath, before negotiating a way back to the roof for both of them. They exchanged terse instructions and grunts of agreement, while making only the most deliberate movements. Lenore had John bend and swing his arms up, so that she could trade the grip on his left leg for two grips of his forearms as he faced inward toward the house. Then she edged slowly back up the roof, pulling him up one inch at a time. When his hands made the level of the ledge itself, she kept pulling until his chest was up to the edge, and then she carefully helped pull him up the rest of the way to safety. Once he was all the way on the roof and away from the edge, while they were still lying down, she wrapped her arms around him. She closed her eyes, buried her face in his neck, and squeezed him tightly.

THE ENTITY HAD no proper name, but that didn't stop millions of beings and thousands of cultures from making ones up for him. He was a creator and sometimes a destroyer, but mostly an explorer, and always an exuberant observer. He generally didn't meddle with the galaxies, worlds, or beings he found or created, preferring instead to sit back and witness events unfolding.

The movements of galaxies, planets and stars were a type of life, too, and he could watch those colorful swirls, explosions, and crashing orbits for eons. Tiny bacteria, massive mammals, colonies of insects, any and all curious or clueless collections of sentient organic matter—even the movements of energy within atoms or in the hearts of supernovas—were all equally entertaining to him. Yes, he actively devoured worlds and beings sometimes, but more often he passively devoured experiences and observations.

Occasionally he *created* life-forms, some in a rough approximation of his image, but mostly driven by the inventive instincts of the moment. His tools were not precise, by any means; creating life to some careful specification was like trying to shape a smooth, round pebble using bolts of lightning or by smashing planets together, like trying to sow a straight line of tiny seeds with mountains for hands. But still, he did it, when the desire arose in him.

When he made life, he would have to go dormant for long periods of time to gather his strength back. His live creations would sometimes flourish, reproduce and expand, battle and build, fall and rise and fall again, seldom lasting more than a few instants in the grand scheme of the entity's vast existence and innumerable works.

Worlds in the immeasurable cosmos could contain life at its hesitant beginnings, or they could host the minuscule, fascinating remnants of creations that were almost entirely gone. Some things just *were*, and the joy was in trying to understand them. Life varied so greatly in intellect, language, shape and size and speed and intent and instinct, isolation and community, longevity of individual life, rate of evolution, and so much more; even common laws of physics could vary under the right circumstances, producing a type of thrilling magic.

He had seen beings spring up from nothing, with no help whatsoever, provided the right combination of elements and luck was present. He had sometimes come upon pockets of existing life—tiny, telltale lights in the titanic void of space—that were the labors of others of his kind, or the handiworks of unknown, absent creators, or the results of inexplicable forces and random coincidence. When this happened, he would approach and closely observe everything, for as long as it took to fathom the totality of the events unfolding there. Sometimes he would watch that life all the way through to its subsequent extinction, and sometimes he would leave it behind and move on to further explorations elsewhere.

The entity had not seen *everything* there was to be seen in all of creation, but he wanted to.

JOHN WASN'T sure how long they lay there on the roof, arms wrapped about each other, letting their heartbeats and breathing slow to normal rates. If there was an accepted amount of time to embrace someone who just miraculously saved you from falling to your death, he felt that they used that measure of time, and then a great deal more. His Majesty nickered from nearby, having not suddenly popped out of existence like so many other misplaced things at the manor, and eventually John and Lenore stood up. John's leg was wobbly from being wrenched against his full weight, but he *was* able to stand. After they stood, Lenore leaned into him again, and even though they were well past the point where they were rocked from their recent adventure over the edge of the roof, he wanted to embrace her for as long as she needed it. After a time, she reached one hand up to the side of his face, and pulled his mouth to hers for a single, sweet kiss.

And then they turned to the house and walked, slowly and

with great care, toward the rooftop stairwell door. He leaned on Lenore as they went past his nearby horse.

John was wondering if he should remove the horse's tack and possibly feed it, when Lenore noticed the peculiar pillar of blue light that John had seen the night before: back behind the house, off in the distance. She immediately stopped walking and stared at it, with her eyebrows pressed suspiciously together. The blood in the corner of her mouth had hardened into a comma. "What in the Maker's name is *that*?" she asked, with a raised voice. Color rose in her face.

"Oh, yeah, *that*," John said. "I saw that last night when I went out to the outhouse."

Lenore started moving quickly to the rooftop door, squinting across the distance to get a look at the huge, strangely illuminated...thing. John thought it could be a structure, or maybe a building? It was like nothing he had seen before, but he was starting to get used to that type of thing around here. If he saw a flying alligator with carnival sparkler-sticks between its toes, streaking across the swirling sky right at that moment, he might hardly remark on it.

Lenore asked, again almost shouting the question, "...but what *is* it?"

"I thought *you* would know. Then again, you typically don't tell me what you know, my lady, so there's usually no point in asking."

Lenore raced down the rooftop stairs to the second-floor landing. She noticed the axe, still stuck in the nearby portrait, and took a moment to wrench it free. The impaled envelope dropped to the floor, leading John's eyes past the small triangle of wall exposed by the misalignment of the painting; he noticed some scratches or marks on the wall there, as Lenore straightened the portrait. She flew down the stairs with the axe in her hands, and he followed. On the porch, she thought of something and stopped, handing the axe to John.

"Here, hold this...and wait a moment." Then she went back in the house while he stood there on the porch, tapping the axe-handle on his hand as if this was just a normal day, slanted horses and flying alligators being as ordinary as anything else in evidence. He didn't know what was happening at the manor this morning, but he did what he had done for most of his time here, which was to simply wait to see what would happen next.

Lenore emerged from the manor carrying an old rifle and some shells. The rifle looked ancient, as likely to blow up in your face as to fire a bullet. She loaded two shells into the side of the housing, said, "Come on," and proceeded around the back of the manor, past the outhouse.

In the scattered trees beyond, perhaps a half mile away across flat ground, a tall spiral of blue light rose from the ground to the dark sky above. Lenore raced toward it as a fierce wind kicked up from the direction of the writhing pillar.

"What *is* it?" John asked, as he jogged along beside her, lugging the awkward axe and working out the muscles in his recently-overstretched legs. He wondered what use the axe would be in an investigation of a strange pillar of glowing light, but carried it along anyway.

Lenore replied, scowling angrily, "I honestly don't know, but I intend to find out."

The wind became stronger as they covered more ground, and John was reminded of the strange weather phenomenon of earlier in the day. It seemed like wind or sunshine could spring up here at the manor, completely out of nowhere. There was an oppressive weight in the air, like the after-effects of a lightning strike; John's ears registered increasing pressure with each stride.

With no attempt to tease her, John said, "But when I asked how much you know about what is going on here at the manor, your note said that you knew '*everything.*'" This was the first time since he had arrived that it seemed Lenore was confused about something happening here.

"Until now, that's true," Lenore said, leaning into the wind, gritting her teeth and breathing quickly. "But this is something else entirely."

The gale was becoming so strong that it was hard to make forward progress. Lenore's long hair was being whipped around by the wind, and when paired with her wild, irate expression, it made her look decidedly unstable. One way of interpreting their previous interactions was that Lenore was unbalanced...a little bit crazy, perhaps from living alone for some extended amount of time. Running alongside her while she belted off toward a blue, tornado-like weather pattern— while she brandished an old rifle—made him think that was the *most likely* interpretation. While he worried over Lenore's stability, he also felt a little silly carrying the axe; the pillar before him was similar to the giant beanstalk in the children's story, and running toward it with the axe made him think that he was playing the role of the silly boy Jacob, running to chop it down before the angry troll could reach the ground.

Lenore was becoming angrier with each stride. She dodged nimbly around bushes and spindly trees, muttering and growling words that John could not make out as they covered ground quickly. Eventually, she shouted, "Why?" and then "Why...are you doing this to us?" John had no idea who she was addressing...what was the point of shouting at the sky? If she was screaming at the blue pillar, what made her think that it could hear at all, or hear her at this distance? Both the beanstalk and the troll in the story were alive, sure, but it was the *troll* that was to be feared. Did Lenore think something was going to climb down the strange pillar?

The ground between them and the pillar had previously been completely flat, but as they progressed, it began to rumble and gradually slope upward. It was as if a mountain was forming right beneath their feet. The top part of the blue funnel was becoming more visible, but that still didn't help John understand what it was: swirling, entwined blue strands of light covering some type of writhing, slick, blue body beneath. It was alive, and it was massive.

Blue strands of light ran along and into the ground, too, like the roots of a giant tree. Though they were still a hundred yards away, these blue "roots" actually reached the very ground they were covering; John saw moving blue protrusions, here and there, making him think of the arms of an octopus, threading through the dirt. With the ground sloping up, it seemed unlikely they would actually reach the center spire.

Lenore stopped near some of the writhing blue bumps and shouted at them, "Why show yourself after all this time?" John looked down at the snaking protrusions and understood why Lenore *thought* it might be hearing her: though only small sections of tentacles were visible, he saw multiple, moving eyes all over them...strange areas, like milky egg whites, each one with three or four corneas jiggling around in them like independent black yolks. Lenore whirled all around with the rifle, and John thought for a moment that she might accidentally shoot him. He held up the hand not holding the axe and asked, "Lenore, what are you doing?"

She leveled the gun at one of the blue projections and suddenly pulled the trigger. The boom of the old rifle was thunderous, echoing all around them for several seconds, along with Lenore's feral screams of rage. Her eyes were darting all around, while her hair whipped across her face in the wind. Her breathing was ragged. The tendrils shifted, below the ground over here, over the ground there, and she shot down toward one of them again. John dropped the axe and moved to her, angling the hot muzzle away with his elbow and reaching to steady her by the shoulder. "Lenore," he said, trying to calm her.

The tendrils sunk beneath the dirt as the angle of the ground became so steep that they would not be able to move any closer, even if they tried running some more. The blue illumination of the funnel in the sky swirled closer to the central pillar, being drawn in like a giant illuminated fishing net. Then there was a bright flash of blue light, a crack of lightning, and the whole pillar plummeted toward the earth, dipping below the lip of the rise in front of them. Like a massive nail being hammered in, all at once, it disappeared from their sight.

Lenore was shaking with emotion, and John wrapped his arms around her. "Lenore," he asked, "what did you think that was?"

She took a few hitching breaths and said quietly, "Nothing new has shown up at the manor for a long time, John." She settled some more and continued, "...something *new* like that... it has to mean that the end is coming."

John didn't like the sound of that one bit. "The end of what?"

They left the gun and the axe where they were, on the slanted ground before the lip of an uncanny crater, and started back toward the manor. She said, "All that is happening to me...to us."

She supported herself on John, slowly regaining her composure as they walked back down to the house.

THAT EVENING, Lenore went up to her room for the night, while John stayed in the parlor. He felt that he would not sleep at all in that cramped back bedroom beyond the cellar stairway, so he didn't even bother going there. He kept a candle burning the whole night while dozing in one of the large, uncomfortable parlor chairs near the fire. When there came whispers and scratching noises in the night, he stifled his soldier's instinct to wake up immediately and investigate, instead willing himself to stay half asleep and pretend that the noises were part of a hazy dream. Eventually, sleep once more took hold, and nothing else occurred. Nobody murdered him in the night, which he took as a small blessing.

In the morning, Lenore came down looking tired, and John noticed some bloody scratches on her left cheek. It looked like someone had raked her face with four long fingernails. John asked about the scratches as she silently pressed a strip of cloth from one of the parlor drawers to her face, but she just shook her head at the question and did not answer.

Lenore used the fireplace grate to prepare some unremarkable green beans for breakfast, which they ate together while sitting in the parlor chairs. Her mood lightened as they ate, and she became more animated with ongoing conversation. They didn't discuss the strange pillar of light from the previous day, or the miracle of the sudden sunshine, or the burned boy on the rooftop. Instead, they negotiated whether or not he would allow her to cut his hair and shave his beard, both of which were noticeably long. She seemed very keen to address this subject, and would not engage on any others. Eventually, he relented, and they brought the needed supplies—a wooden chair and one of the baskets from their shared bathing of the day before—out to the yard. The weather was as it always was: overcast, with the sun shrouded by clouds and apparently only available if someone took the trouble to perform a draining, and altogether disturbing, magical charm. The town of River's Edge, visible off in the distance, still showed signs of some recent fires.

Lenore positioned the chair with its back to the river and motioned John into it. She covered his chest and shoulders with one of the brown towels and gave him a hand-mirror – "in case you want to check my work," she said. When she began combing and trimming his hair, it was with no hesitation whatsoever. It became clear in a few moments that Lenore knew exactly what she was doing.

John watched the morning fog roll lazily over the gloomy grounds, scanning the many windows of Everbridge Manor in case one of the other "residents" decided to make an appearance. He wondered if the encounter with Kitty was supposed to tell him something, or if the strange glowing pillar behind the mansion was part of some larger puzzle. Why was the little boy —whom John did not recognize at all—trying to hurt him? The river drifted by behind them, toward town; John watched it in the mirror when he raised it every once in a while, to see what Lenore was doing to his hair.

John saw His Majesty, walking far beyond the back of the house, still wearing his saddle, and it reminded him of some responsibilities he had neglected. "Oh, there's His Majesty again. I feel terrible that I haven't bothered to find something to feed him—or even remove his saddle!—since I've been here. Have you, perhaps, been—"

"Don't worry about it, John," Lenore replied. "He'll be just fine, no care or feeding required. That horse will outlive both of us."

John wasn't sure he agreed, but he decided to let it go. After a few more moments, he caught a glimpse of the town in the mirror and remarked, "I wonder what type of fire has happened in River's Edge, if everybody is safe." Lenore continued to work, but did not comment. "That town has terrible luck," he continued. "I remember a fire happening there, back when I was a young boy."

"Yes," Lenore replied. "I remember that fire, too."

"Oh? From when you were a girl? I think I was around five or six when it happened."

"I'm sure you'll see what's happening there, eventually...it is highly likely, in fact. But you're right that the town has bad luck."

He shook his head, and said, "I truly don't know what to make of this place, Lenore." She reached her hand to his chin and stopped it from swiveling as she worked on his hair. She was now lifting small sections of hair from the top of his head in between her fingers and expertly trimming them. Her scissors moved so quickly that John felt a flutter of nervousness. "When you figure it out," she said, "I'm sure you'll let me know what you've gleaned."

"I will, I will...but sometimes it's difficult to believe all of the things I have seen." He checked her progress on his hair, and was astounded that she was working quickly and with more skill and artistry than he had ever seen. It seemed like she wasn't even trying, but she was clearly in the process of giving him the best haircut he had received in his life. "This amazing haircut, as just one example! Didn't you say that you were a schoolteacher, Lenore? You didn't mention a career as a hair-dresser!"

"'Perfection through practice,' as the saying goes," she replied, but did not elaborate any further. She combed the back of his hair down and clipped along the hairline at the back of his neck.

A few minutes later, the haircut was done, with no further comment on her uncanny hairdressing ability. Lenore moved on to shaving his beard. Before attending to it with the large, sharp, straight-razor, she slathered his face with a scratchy, herbed lotion that smelled of rosemary. "Another home-made concoction?" he asked, and she just nodded before going to work on his beard with the razor. Again, it became clear that she was an expert in the undertaking.

Lenore worked silently, and John eventually returned to his musings on the strangeness of his time at the manor: "A sane person doesn't believe in vengeful spirits or magical spells, but I have seen both of those things here...with my own eyes. Either I am losing my grip, or these grounds are under some kind of curse." He paused for a few moments to consider this. "Yes, I fear that Everbridge Manor is a place cursed with an evil magic."

"That's not wrong, Raindrop," Lenore said. In the handheld mirror, John saw her smile mischievously and move her face close to his head. "No, it's not wrong at all. But it is also a place of haircuts...and stolen kisses." She laughed and leaned in from behind and kissed him softly on the temple.

He closed his eyes, partly to concentrate on arranging his thoughts about the evil events all around them, but also to let the gentle touch of her lips linger. "As pleasant as that is, please don't distract me, Lenore – I'm trying to understand what this all means."

"And that's what I'm telling you, my love. That kiss wasn't just a distraction...it's as much an answer to these questions as I have. It's best not to focus on the painful parts, as much as they constantly intrude."

"Philosopher, mind-reader, predicter of the future, dubious summoner of uncanny weather patterns, hairdresser, barber. You have many talents."

"Thank you! That is a complimentary list, but I believe you have overlooked my skill as a cook."

"Entirely on purpose."

"You do realize that I am holding a sharp object near your throat right now, don't you, John?"

He laughed, but then flashed on "she is a murderer" in his head, and abruptly stopped smiling. Her straight-razor was indeed long, and extremely sharp. Lenore stopped smiling as well. "See?" she said sadly, gazing back at the river behind them. "Even our lighthearted moments must be stolen...and they can be stolen back, too."

Behind them, John noticed something strange in the river, reflected in his hand-mirror. He started to crane around to see it, but Lenore gently held his face straight ahead. "Don't look, John. We don't need to take the bait every time it is cast."

Instead of turning, he looked in the mirror as she continued his shave. Two things were happening in the river behind them. First, there were several blackened bodies floating slowly downstream, trailing wispy tendrils of steam, smoke, and a dreadful smell as they passed. There were at least six dead people, of various sizes; John angled the mirror around and noticed one child-shape, one large adult shape, and several in between. These burned people were not moving, as they were clearly dead. They simply drifted along, sad and silent lumps of flesh drifting behind the wooden chair that they had set up for John's haircut and shave. The second remarkable thing took a moment to figure out, with the view in the mirror being backwards as it was: the river, which normally flowed *toward* River's Edge, was now running in the opposite direction.

"Yes," Lenore said quietly, still making sure John did not turn around. "Our river is going the wrong way, my love. But if we wait a few moments, it will be back to normal."

John said, "...but those bodies...in the river...how can anything be considered normal, when *that* can happen?"

The last of the floating bodies sailed beyond the view of the hand-mirror, and John considered the spectacle. Eventually, he stated the obvious: "It's like the universe it trying to tell us something."

Lenore smiled and patted his shoulder tenderly. "Maybe the universe is telling us to be happy that we weren't in the bathing pool just now?"

She wiped John's face off with a cloth, saying, "All done." He looked toward the river and knew that she was referring both to the shave and the disturbing incident that had just played out behind them. The river was now flowing *toward* town, as it always had.

"When I was a teenager," John said, upon considering what

had just happened, "I sometimes used to go to the Harvest Festival in River's Edge. Do you remember it, in the Fall? They set it up in one of the clearings beyond the school, all pumpkins and baked goods and a frivolous parade with the town elders and the fire brigade."

"I've heard about that before, yes," Lenore said. They began to carry the chair and supplies back to the house.

"One year," John continued, "one of the farmers set up a haunted corn maze."

"Oh!" Lenore interrupted. "I wish *we* had a haunted corn maze."

"For heaven's sake," he laughed. "Why?"

"Well, fresh corn on the cob, for one thing!" She rubbed her hand absently across the scratches on her face. "And for another, maybe we could consign all of our scary things to the official haunted corn maze, and not have to encounter them as we go about our normal days!"

"Good idea!" he replied. "Well, anyway, I bring it up because the scary things in that corn maze from my youth remind me of what the universe seems to be parading before us here: some skinny guy dressed up like a scarecrow, carrying a pitchfork and popping out at you from a side alley...the town butcher madly chasing you with a cleaver, his apron all spattered with blood."

They set the grooming supplies inside and walked back out to the porch to continue talking.

Lenore observed, "I can't really talk to you about it, but maybe the universe thinks that kind of thing scares you the most."

"Perhaps so," John said. He continued, in a low whisper, "But the thing is, while a haunted corn maze is chilling in its own way—I mean, who *doesn't* get scared when someone grabs their arm from out of nowhere in a dark labyrinth, right?—that kind of thing is just not as scary to me as it was when I was a teen."

Lenore leaned close to listen, taking one of his hands in hers and saying, "Oh?"

"My experiences in the war...well, I guess they changed my opinion of what is terrifying. The man in the skeleton suit in the corn maze is nothing, really, when compared with the real prospect of being maimed on the battlefield, or having all of your friends die right next to you."

"That counts as a blessing, then," Lenore said. "Be thankful that the universe didn't figure out that distinction. But consider this: the bloody butcher in the corn maze wasn't allowed to actually kill you with his cleaver, correct?"

John laughed. "Of course not! It's just for show!"

"Well, maybe the haunted corn maze we have here is scarier than you think."

ACROSS THE EVERBRIDGE, along the path coming from Junction City, they noticed a wagon moving toward the manor. It was being pulled by a single horse, and some low boxes were visible in the wagon's bed.

Lenore said, "Oh look, it's Cartwright, come to appeal to your sense of honor and deliver our supplies. How will he possibly avoid giving us the yeast, sugar, salt, and steaks that were previously requested?"

A small man was driving the cart, with another man sitting right next to him. John noticed that the two men had the same body shape, and wore the same clothes.

"Who is that with him?" Lenore asked, suddenly becoming serious.

John sighed. "And how should I know that, Lenore?"

She began to walk briskly toward the bridge, newfound agitation in her every step. "He's never come here with anybody else before." Ten seconds later, they stood beside the wagon, looking up at the driver and his odd passenger. The driver, presumably Cartwright, was a short, balding man with small round spectacles, brown work-pants, a white button-down shirt, and a brown vest. The passenger looked just like him, down to wearing exactly the same clothes and glasses, but had a distinct manner of distraction that the driver lacked. The passenger was squinting and swiveling his head all around, as if he was having trouble with his vision.

"Good afternoon—" Cartwright began, before Lenore cut him off, ignoring him and addressing the passenger.

"Who are you?" she demanded angrily. John found her reaction remarkably similar to her reaction to the strange blue spiral the previous evening: slightly unhinged. He wondered if she would run off for the axe or gun, but then remembered that, last night, they had left them in the trees beyond the outhouse.

The passenger did not look at her, instead continuing to swivel his head, as if testing it. His nose twitched, lifting and lowering the spectacles. They could hear his breathing, slow and hitching, with an uneven rhythm. There was something unhealthy, unsettled, about this man who was clearly Cartwright's twin brother. The twin did not answer Lenore's question, so she instead addressed Cartwright: "Who is this man?" she demanded.

Cartwright looked over and seemed as confused about the passenger as Lenore was. "I don't know," he said. "I've never seen him before in my life."

Since the passenger looked exactly like Cartwright, this seemed rather hard for John to believe. Lenore looked like she was going to climb up onto the cart and start throttling the twin for her answers.

"Are we supposed to believe he's your twin brother or something?"

Cartwright shook his head. "I...I don't know."

"Why is he on the cart with you?"

"I'm sure I can't say."

Lenore was furious at the man's unhelpful responses, which made John laugh before he could stop himself. He was remembering the night with the foul tea and the crazy kitchen-smashing matron where Lenore gave him these same kinds of answers to John's every question. His laughter only made Lenore *more* irate.

"Do you have something you want to share with the class, John?" she asked.

He smiled. "Well, I'm sure I can't say."

The passenger's breathing was so uneven that John wondered if the twin was getting enough oxygen. The man grabbed the top collar of his white shirt, pulling it away from his throat for a moment. As he did this, both Lenore and John clearly saw some of the skin on the man's chest beneath the shirt; it was the same striking blue hue as the strange spiral in the sky from the previous night. Before John could wonder if the man was blue due to lack of oxygen, he also noticed, in that brief glimpse, a few circular white patches, with glistening dots moving around in them, like eyeballs with multiple pupils.

John was so surprised by this strange sight that couldn't keep himself from saying, "Good heavens!"

Cartwright did his best to ignore all this as he slowly drove the cart over the bridge into the courtyard of the manor. The passenger seemed to figure out his breathing problem, but continued to look around incredulously and without any specific focus. He held up his hands in front of his face, scrutinizing them at various distances, as if he had never seen them before.

"Let's get down to our business, Lenore," Cartwright said, squinting down at a small piece of paper he held. He selected a bag from the boxes and bags at the front of the cart. "Last time, madam, there was an order for yeast...so here are your potatoes." He handed John the cloth bag, containing three medium-sized, brown potatoes. John did not consider himself a genius, but he was smart enough to know the difference between yeast and potatoes, and said so. "These...these are...potatoes," he said.

"Yes, *yeast*. That was the order, correct? And as for the sugar, here is some mint." A moment later, John was holding three bunches of green mint-stalks, each somewhat wilted and bound with string. He looked quizzically at the herbs, then back at Cartwright, and eventually made to hand the bunches back to the man, but Lenore reached over and took them roughly from him instead. "Don't give that back, John! We can use *mint*, even if it's not actually sugar."

"It *is* sugar," Cartwright announced. "Just as you requested."

Lenore continued to eye the strange twin while Cartwright delivered his goods. The twin was looking at the gray sky, first with his round spectacles on, and then again with them off. A thick line of drool ran from the corner of his mouth, which he seemed not to notice in any way. While the twin continued testing the effects of his glasses, Cartwright continued to work down the list of items previously requisitioned, always providing something entirely different from the order but grandly declaring that it was exactly as requested. For salt, he gave two squishy coconuts. For steaks, he gave a loose handful of pistachio nuts, which John struggled to hold, along with the potatoes and coconuts, without dropping all of it over the stones of the yard. Lastly, Cartwright handed down a box of simple supplies, which Lenore accepted: four small bags, containing variously: flour, wheat, dried white beans, and radishes. Cartwright inexplicably referred to the box by an *accurate* name by saying, "Lastly, here are some more supplies."

He then asked what they would like for the next delivery, and Lenore turned her attention to Cartwright. She asked him for coffee beans, yams, eggplant, and bananas. With no attempt to hide the conversation from Cartwright, she said, "He won't bring any of those, but I like to ask for different things for the fun of it. Eventually, he's going to accidentally bring me sugar when I ask for yellow squash, and then I shall rejoice."

Cartwright looked confused. "I always fulfill your orders, madam, quite accurately, I might say."

"I'll beat you some day, little man," Lenore said quietly, without any anger. She turned her attention back to scrutinizing the twin, as John wondered what she thought that strange man signified.

He noticed, without remarking on it, that Lenore was apparently not paying for these goods—wrong as they were, based on what was ordered—and that Cartwright did not request payment from her either. Of this transaction, he supposed that a lack of payment was the least unusual thing about it.

Lenore asked John what he wanted to order, and John immediately thought that he might like a steak...but that didn't seem likely to work out. He then considered responding by saying that he would probably not be here at the manor upon their next visit...but after another moment's hesitation, he just asked for fresh corn on the cob and bacon. Some bacon would truly be nice.

"Certainly, sir," Cartwright asserted. "You shall have them, on my next delivery. And how are you doing with the commission? Have you determined what happened in River's Edge?"

"Pardon me? Commission?"

"Yes, the agreement we made, sir, before you left Junction City a month ago? You accepted payment to investigate some incidents over in the town?" He nodded toward River's Edge, which continued to smolder under twin trails of smoke. "Very troubling, but we must get to the bottom of it." John looked confused, so Cartwright clarified by pointing very clearly toward the town. "Just over there?"

"Yes, I know the town, but I remember no such conversation."

"Well that can hardly be the case, sir. You are an investigator, after all, and you accepted the commission...signed the paperwork. The sum was considerable."

John had no recollection of any such agreement, and told Cartwright so. Cartwright looked annoyed, rummaging in some boxes at his feet, saying, "Look. I have the documentation... hold on, the documentation...somewhere..." The twin looked down at the boxes, and then over at Lenore and John; John thought for a second that the twin had some kind of disability, but then remembered the blue skin and the eyeballs; *disability* didn't seem like the right word at all, though John couldn't discern the right one at that moment.

Cartwright patted the pockets of his vest, and then exclaimed, "Ah! Here it is."

He pulled a folded envelope from his left vest pocket, flattening it out. The twin reached over absently, as if interested in taking the envelope himself, but Cartwright leaned away with some irritation and handed it down to John. "This is our agreement. An *official* agreement. If you are a man of honor, you'd best get to it." John recognized it immediately: the Junction City seal was on the outside of the envelope, and his name was written on the front in an official script. John looked over at Lenore, who crossed her arms and raised an eyebrow, but said nothing.

"Well, aren't you going to open it?" Cartwright asked sharply. He looked like someone who ordered a nice steak, but has been served pistachio nuts instead.

John opened the envelope. There were two pieces of paper inside: a contract for services, signed by Cartwright and John himself, and a stamped deposit record from the Bank of Junction City. Both documents looked entirely genuine, though John felt he had never seen either before.

It was Cartwright's turn to regard John with severely folded arms. The twin saw this and tried to wind his own arms into the same gesture, but couldn't find the right order or placement, fussing with a frown and giving up after a few tries.

"Do you find everything in order?" Cartwright asked.

The contract was an agreement between John and the government of Junction City to conduct an inquiry into the current circumstances in the town of River's Edge. John recognized his own signature, on both the contract and the record of deposit. The sum was quite substantial indeed, amounting as it did to a full year of John's normal salary as a city constable.

John thought about the gap in his memory, from the moment that he was considering leaving Junction City to the moment that he showed up at Everbridge Manor with some grave injuries. It *was* possible that he had been engaged to an official inquiry before leaving the city. The bank paperwork showed a balance that *seemed* correct, after being increased by the significant amount of money quantified on both documents. He wondered if he had gone to River's Edge already, in his official capacity, without remembering it. Perhaps he had somehow become injured during the investigation? That might explain how he ended up here on Lenore's doorstep—correction, on *Kitty's* doorstep—so near to River's Edge...perhaps when His Majesty departed the scene of some altercation over there.

"So, will you do it?" Cartwright asked.

John looked over at Lenore, who was shaking her head slowly. John had to admit that he was tremendously curious about the conditions in the town. And regardless of Lenore's obvious objections, he did not wish to agree to a job, be paid in advance for it, and then not do it.

He said, "Yes, I'll do it."

Cartwright looked pleased, as if all was right with the world again. "Excellent. I'll expect a full report."

Lenore lifted up the box of food staples and said, "Yes, yes, now that we've done all that, I'm sure you and your beloved twin brother have other duties to attend to, Cartwright, such as finding a way to sort the deliveries so that we might get the things we order."

"But I always—"

Lenore interrupted, waving a dismissive hand, saying, "So sorry that you must be going, but you must be going." Then she turned away and began carrying her box toward the manor.

Cartwright mumbled, "Why, yes..." and started to turn the cart around in the courtyard before the house. John, not wanting to follow the apparent trend of being rude to their visitors, said, "Good day, sirs, and thank you for the steaks." And then he added, "I'll see to your commission shortly."

INSIDE, John and Lenore transferred their small delivery to pantry baskets in the decimated kitchen, saying nothing. The light from the fire in the other room was barely sufficient for the task, but then again there were so few items that the lack of light barely impeded them. They ate the handful of pistachios as they worked. Lenore didn't seem mad about his agreement to Cartwright's proposition, but rather, looked resigned to an unpleasant task that has presented itself. John was sure that this was the result of his agreement to help Cartwright. He knew that firm, tight-lipped expression from his compatriots in the militia, when they were ordered to patrol a dangerous area or assume a tactical battlefield position that was likely to get most of the company killed. There was none of the playful conversation that passed while she groomed him in the yard.

"You know that I was planning to go to town, anyway," he started, but she put up a hand to stop him.

"It's all right, John, you don't need to explain. It's unreasonable to hope that you would ignore a job that was supposedly paid for in advance. I understand your decision, and know that I'll help you in any way I can."

"What did you think was going on with Cartwright's twin?"

"If it is who I think it is, he has some nerve showing up here after all this time," she replied cryptically. "But in any case, it is something *new*, related to that strange blue tornado we saw last night, as you probably saw." John nodded, shuddering at the thought of somebody with all those eyeballs on their chest. Lenore continued, "New things are...well, they are unexpected around here."

John walked out to the parlor to sit in one of the tall chairs near the fire, hoping that she would come to keep him company and discuss it further. Instead, she said, "I've told you that I don't sleep well at night, and I confess that I am somewhat tired now. I might go up to close my eyes for a moment, if you don't mind."

"Not a bit, Lenore," he said. "Sleep well." And she headed out to the entry and up the stairs. John sat and enjoyed the fire for some time, considering the prospect of picking out a book from one of the nearby shelves and scanning through it. He was, however, no reader, and so he simply sat in the warmth and closed his own eyes.

JOHN BEGAN TO DREAM, in the way of most of his dreams at the manor: so real as to feel like he was actually experiencing the events of the dream first-hand. Every sound in the dream was crisp and distinct, every thought in his head was the thought he had during the time period being visualized.

Perhaps because he had seen her spirit the day before, beckoning to him from the very chair in which he now slept, John dreamt of—and remembered—the last day he had seen his mother, when he was just five years old. For all of those five years, he and his mother lived together in a small, uncomfortable room behind the cobbler's shop in Junction City, which she could scarcely afford. He would often be in the room alone, entertaining himself for hours with wooden blocks that he pretended were soldiers participating in imaginary battles, while his mother did whatever single mothers did to earn a few coins each day in the big city. She never told him what her job was, if she had one at all, and he was not old enough to think to ask. The grizzled cobbler seemed overly-friendly to his mother, which was perhaps why the man let them stay in his back room.

One afternoon, John's mother burst into their room, visibly upset, muttering that she had found "that rat" and that she intended to get back what had been taken from her. By "that rat," John knew immediately that she meant her husband—his father—who had run off when he learned that his mother was pregnant, leaving her with no money and sticking her with the bill for the rent on the apartment the couple had been living in at the time.

John's mother quickly put on her most-serviceable clothes: a dusky, ruffled dress that was threadbare in places, but had the best mendings of anything she owned. She then threw her remaining belongings—and John's as well—into a sack. It didn't take long to gather up almost everything they owned. She yanked John by the hand, and within five minutes of her agitated arrival to the room behind the cobbler's shop, the two of them were on the road. It would be five years before John returned to Junction City. "Your lousy father is just over in River's Edge, John," his mother fumed, the sack of their possessions bouncing over her shoulder. "Can you believe that? He's been there this whole time!"

John had spent all five of his years in Junction City and had never been outside of the city limits. River's Edge might as well have been in another country altogether, because he could not comprehend anything further away than Church Row on one side of the city or the docks on the other. The two of them walked for a few hours as morning turned into afternoon. His mother hauled him along by his hand, moving at a high, excited clip, rambling on about how she was still married to that louse and that she would make him remember his obligation to his wife and his son, if it was the last thing she ever did. She had their certificate of marriage in the front pocket of her skirt and intended to wave it in his fat face to get what she wanted. Apparently, her husband now lived in a mansion outside of River's Edge—"a *mansion,* of all things!" she exclaimed—and as they walked down the road, it didn't take her very long to make plans for her and her son to *live* in that mansion, regardless of what her worthless, runaway spouse wanted.

A kind man, riding in a cart that was pulled by a single horse, was heading in the same direction as John and his mother, and he offered to let them ride with him. He said his name was Rolf, explaining that he was a constable in Junction City, making one of his monthly trips to River's Edge to deliver and retrieve the official town and police paperwork that was needed to keep their district running. Sometimes he would work a day or two in the station over there in River's Edge, he told them, adding that he would stay the night in the inn across the street from the school-house. Rolf knew of John's father, after he heard John's mother describing the man, using the most derogatory terms she could manage. Rolf explained that John's father was now a busi-nessman in town who kept contracts with loggers, miners, fishermen, and farmers around the district to store their goods and deliver them where they needed to go. "A professional middle-man," is how Rolf described John's father, "...always a bit full of himself, if I can say so." This characterization fit exactly into what John's mother thought of her wayward spouse, and she agreed that, yes, Rolf could say so. Apparently, John's father no longer went by his given name, which was "Bertram," instead expecting everyone in town to call him "The Master."

Rolf also knew of the mansion that John's mother described, and offered to drop the two of them off there. When they talked about the mansion, Rolf suddenly appeared to remember something, but did not say what he was thinking. His brow wrinkled and his mouth became a pursed line, and he then offered to accompany John and his mother right to the front door, muttering, "in case there's trouble." But John's mother had her own plans at this point, and said that a police escort was "so very kind, sir," but unnecessary. John chuckled at the thought that she probably planned to smack "The Master" over his head with a frying pan, and did not want a constable present to witness her intended assault.

The trio had been travelling with the river on their left and dense forest on their right for a few hours as the sun began to go down in the sky, when next they came upon a bridge across the river. The bridge was more functional than decorative, with a simple wooden cover shading it against the afternoon sun. Beyond the bridge, there was an ornate, two-story mansion, ensconced in a cobbled courtyard and surrounded by robust trees and bushes. "I believe they call it 'Everbridge Manor,'" Rolf said, slowing the wagon near the road-side edge of the bridge.

In the courtyard outside the manor, there was an old oak stump with an axe buried in it, as well as a vegetable patch over which a tall scarecrow presided. The scarecrow wore an old straw hat and a giant white shirt that flapped ominously in the breeze. The mansion itself had a wide porch on one side, tall windows all around, and a high, gabled roof. John's mother gasped as she saw all of this, hopping down from the wagon in an excited hurry. She grabbed John and her bag, and briskly thanked Rolf for the ride before hustling across the bridge. Rolf called to them, "I'll be in town at the station, ma'am, if you need me," and young John noted some real concern in the man's voice, which his mother completely ignored.

A WOMAN'S voice awoke him from his dream, saying, "John. John." It was Kitty, standing in the dark in the murky entry hallway.

"Kitty?" he asked, somewhat groggy at being yanked from his realistic dream-memory of standing on the porch of this very house, with his mother, twenty-five years earlier. He tried, but could not remember what happened after she knocked on the door.

Kitty turned and walked down the back hallway. "Yes, this way."

There was no light from anything except the fireplace, so John lit a small, nearby candle in the fire and carried it with him. Walking to the entry and around to the hallway, he saw Kitty disappearing to the right, down the cellar stair. She said, "In here, John."

When he looked down the stairwell, it was completely dark and completely empty. Kitty was not waiting for him on the stairs. The stinging smell of kerosene was emanating from down there, and he could hear something dripping...heavy drops falling into a large body of liquid. The candle-light barely illuminated the first four steps, and there was an echoing blackness beyond. John's survival senses were on high alert, and he was having some trouble willing his feet to move beyond the threshold. A chill worked its way up his back to his neck, making the hairs along that path stand on end for a moment. The grandfather clock ticked behind him; he promised himself that if it bonged its hourly chime right at that moment, he would not go jumping down the stairs.

Every time he had gone chasing after one of the other people in the house—the *spirits*, his mind interjected—something unpleasant had occurred. Lenore had said that they didn't need to take the bait every time the line was cast, and there was probably wisdom in that. He considered a tactical retreat...ignoring his sister's appearance entirely, perhaps even going so far as to find Lenore to ask again about the foreboding basement. And that lead to a thought of what he would do *instead* of investigating the basement and confronting his sister: sitting serenely by the fire with Lenore and sipping some of her awful tea, so safe and pleasant, and he felt momentarily ashamed at that imagined act of cowardice. Yes, he had been afraid of this dark space and its unpleasant smells when he was little, but he was no longer little.

He held his candle up in front of himself and stepped into the narrow stairwell, walking down each step carefully, trying to be aware of what might happen in front or from behind. For balance, he pressed his right hand against the wet, side wall, which compressed inward with the consistency of oil-soaked newspapers.

When John directed the candle upwards, a tall man with a bowler hat stepped down to the top of the stairs. His shape filled the entire doorway above. It was Rooster, grinning and showing his dirty teeth.

John was three-quarters of the way down the stairs when Rooster came rushing down at him. Though ready for just such an attack, John had little to work with at the bottom of a long, straight stairwell, against a man who was six inches taller and running at full speed. John squared his feet to maintain his balance.

Without a word, Rooster covered the entire distance in three large, pounding steps. When he was close enough, John hammered the man's face with his right fist, a sound shot that cracked something beneath Rooster's eye. But the tall man had flown down the stairway with no regard for the safety of either of them, and the two of them crashed together and plummeted roughly down the remainder of the stairs. John's candle was knocked from his grip and—quite luckily—winked out against the stairwell wall as the grappling pair slammed to the basement floor in complete darkness.

The fall was less jarring than it otherwise would have been, because the basement was actually a pool of kerosene, at least a foot deep. There was something rough and sharp on the floor, in the liquid; John thought it might be shards of glass. His head and his face were initially submerged, and he thrashed up and out, kicking at the man above him and coughing as the unexpected liquid scorched his mouth and nose and throat. The kerosene had gotten in John's eyes when he had been submerged, and he pressed them shut against a burning pain. He punched at Rooster's arms and shoulders, driving an elbow across what felt like a forehead or temple. After a few more moments of flailing and bashing, the tall man suddenly withdrew. For a few moments, there was silence, and John pushed himself up on his knees, coughing and gasping and trying to avoid the large glass shards that threatened to cut his arms and hands. Then, he heard movement around him, abrupt splashes and rapid breathing, from several directions. It was hard to tell which direction to face, to be ready for another assault. The sounds were all around.

Something big smashed into his shoulder, knocking John back down into the kerosene pool. A gruff voice that John did not recognize growled, "What is the meaning of this?" and then the speaker moved off, shouting, "You have *no power* here!"

What sounded like a heavy boot came crashing down right next to John's lowered head, splashing kerosene up into his nose. Had the boot been six inches closer, John's head would have been smashed flat on the concrete floor at the bottom of the pool. Rooster shouted, "Now look what you've gone and done, Johnny!" and he, too, moved away, barking, "This is a real mess."

There were several people close now, perhaps four or five, frantically pressing into John, crushing him, and also outwardly beating on him with fists and booted feet. John held up his arms to deflect the various attacks. He could hear the sound of the little boy, chuckling and snickering, off to one side. After another punch from Rooster or one of the others here rocked the side of his head, John decided he had to make it back to the stairs...though he was completely turned around as to where the stairs were. People were being pressed against his head and sides; his face kept getting knocked around, sometimes submerging in the caustic liquid. His arms and hips and knees were being cut up from the glass. He was losing this fight; there were too many attackers, and the lack of light was a fatal disadvantage. John felt a bony shape that he thought might be the innkeeper woman pressing down on his legs, and another ample figure wrenching his shoulder that was probably the angry matron. As he warded off blows and shoved away crushing bodies that encroached from all sides, John heard the scrape of a something metal against a tin can nearby, as an unfamiliar man's voice purred, "Mmm. Peaches."

No longer able to strike out with any force of his own, John was reeling. He inched toward an edge of the room, hoping to only face attackers from a single side. A few feet away, across the room from the voice of the fruit lover, Kitty asked, "What have you done, John?"

And suddenly, the room was flooded with light, as a dozen candles, high up on the walls, lit at once. Except for John, there was nobody in the basement.

John gaped up at the room around him with amazement. He needed to get out of here quickly; the fumes from the kerosene in the room were burning and poisoning his lungs, but he stayed where he was, not understanding what his stinging eyes were showing him. With twelve candles burning, he could see the whole space in vibrant detail. When John had asked Lenore, "What is in the basement?" she had given him her answer on the violet paper: "Kerosene in glass jars, and candles. Lots of kerosene." This was strictly correct, but it just left *so much out*, that it was no real answer at all.

The basement was nothing like the dark, disused, low-ceilinged space he remembered. When he had lived here with his Aunt Agnes and Kitty, this had been a cramped, dirt-floored storage area where his Aunt sometimes kept—and forgot about—shelves and baskets of vegetables. By neglecting her collection, the vegetables remained in the basement far past the threshold where they were edible; during certain times of year, with no door available to close, the smell of the rotting organic matter made it all the way to John's bedroom.

This basement room was some kind of bizarre shrine, not a root cellar. It was much larger than the space he remembered, perhaps fifteen feet square and ten feet tall. Like the rest of the manor, the walls here were made of wood, but these were all painted a dazzling white, though some elaborate artwork had been rendered along the top portion of all the walls. The ceiling was painted—with astounding realism—to look like the roiling gray skies outside the manor. The floor was not dirt; it was made from a smooth black stone. John wasn't wrong about what he had surmised while sloshing around the room, fighting in the dark: the whole space was foot-deep in kerosene, and now the source of that kerosene was abundantly clear.

When he saw it, he knew he needed to get out of here immediately, leave the manor entirely, in fact...but he was so amazed at what he was seeing that he took a few moments before he moved toward the stairwell.

In each corner of the room was a giant, round, glass jar, filled to the top with the same clear, yellowish fuel oil that he was now standing in up to his shins. The jars looked exactly like the kind his Aunt would sometimes use for preserving jam, complete with thick glass and a metal screw-on top, but they were completely out of proportion to normal canning jars, each one standing taller than John himself. One jar had been smashed to pieces, with only the bottom six inches of broken glass remaining, which accounted for the lacerating shards and crystals submerged on the floor.

If a room with four giant jelly jars of kerosene wasn't disturbing enough, the paintings around the top of the walls were even more bizarre. John wondered if Lenore had painted them; she was unexpectedly skilled as a hairdresser and a barber, so there was no reason to suspect that she was not also a talented artist with paint. But if Lenore had constructed this room, had painted this ritualistic banner around the tops of the walls, he had great reason to fear for her sanity.

One side of the room showed two scenes of life on the grounds of Everbridge Manor, complete with the gray weather pattern swirling above. Above the smashed jelly jar, the clouds were parted, showing brilliant orange sunshine, the rays gleaming majestically onto the ground below. The mural continued around to the next corner, culminating in a windy, cryptic scene above a jelly jar: a mysterious woman holding a swaddled child in her arms; the woman's long, black hair was blowing across her face, obscuring it. On the other side of the room, the scene grew smoky and fiery, with flames and glowing, floating embers dominating the two remaining corners and the wall in between them. There were burning buildings all around on that side of the room. Above one jar, a man stood in the flames holding an axe. His face and body were completely in shadow, but he was a fearsome figure to behold...crafted with angry black brush-stokes, a red glow around his whole body. Dark figures of various shapes and sizes surrounded the terrible figure of the man. These dark figures wore hooded cloaks, with the faces in the hoods drawn as barely-discernable skulls. The last corner, which also had a giant kerosene jar in it, was very similar to the dark man's corner. In this case, however, it was a *woman* standing in the fire, all in shadow, yet glowing; the woman, similarly surrounded by dark figures with hooded skulls, was holding a small, thin blade.

John had seen enough. He could barely breathe with the heavy fumes in the air, and he thought to himself that it was a complete miracle that the whole manor did not explode immediately, with the combination of the fumes, this pooled, flammable liquid, and twelve tall candles alight nearby. He rushed up the stairs, intending to find Lenore and get both of them out immediately. When he made the landing, he turned left toward the front door. A hand grabbed him on the shoulder from behind, startling him, and he whirled to see Lenore standing there, a look of concern on her face upon seeing the blood on his hands and arms, and his oil-slick hair. "John, are you all right?"

"Lenore!" he shouted. He had become frantic from the fight in the basement and the strange revelation shown by the candles below. "We have to...we have to leave—there's a giant pool of kerosene in the basement!"

She put both hands on his shoulders, saying, "Yes, I know. Calm down. Let me look at your arms."

"No! We're standing on top of...some kind of...bomb! Please, Lenore...if we stay here, we will surely be killed!"

From the basement doorway, John heard the low rumbling sound that had occurred when he and Lenore spoke previously.

It was as if some giant containers of liquid were vibrating, and John now had a good idea just which containers those were. She had called the sound "a warning," and John was starting to understand part of what that meant. Lenore heard the sound, too, and she took a deep breath, speaking carefully. "I know what you saw down there, John." From below, there came the *tink-tink* sound, a metal object such as the head of the axe being tapped on one of the jars in the basement. "But we can't go anywhere."

The rumble increased. John said, "What do you mean? We can *walk* to River's Edge...or ride to Junction City or Four Corners, or the others—some of those places are within a half-day by horseback! We need to get out of here!"

"Let's go outside and talk. I'll see to your arms, but I need a few supplies first." She led him to the kitchen, where she took a clean dishtowel from a drawer, and then filled a bucket of water from the pump there. Next, they went out to the porch, where Lenore lifted his cut arms to look at them. "This isn't far enough," he said gravely, and they moved further away from the house to the middle of the courtyard. The clouds out here were ominous; it looked like it would rain soon.

When they were far enough away that John felt they would not be killed by the imminent explosion, Lenore started to pick out some shards of glass from his arms, saying nothing as she worked with the towel and the water.

He asked, "Do you have nothing to say of the giant jars of kerosene in the basement, Lenore?"

"I wish I could, my love, but you will have to draw your own conclusions."

"I conclude that living above that much flammable liquid is insanity itself, Lenore, but you know that already." She gave no indication of agreement, and he continued by asking, "Are those your murals down there, your jars, your candles? Is that *me* drawn in that painting?"

"I did not paint, fill, or light anything down there, if that helps you. But I can say no more about it."

"You *cannot* say, or you *will not* say?"

She sighed. "Do you really want to play word games with the schoolteacher, John? Or for that matter, vex an accused witch?"

"Surely, the question isn't all that vexing, and you're no more a witch than I am a penguin. You're still not going to answer it?"

"It's both, if you must know. I *cannot*, and I also *will not*, speak to you about the condition of the basement—or of the house, for that matter. For that, Raindrop, you have my apologies."

It was John's turn to sigh. He looked at the front of manor and then over at the small town visible in the distance beyond. Two lazy pillars of smoke rose from River's Edge to the dark sky. "Then I'll go to River's Edge. There must be some answers there."

Lenore nodded. "You're right about that, but can it wait until tomorrow? I was planning to roast up those potatoes with the mint that Cartwright gave us. It isn't much, but it seems like it would be tastier than what we've been eating recently, don't you think?"

The house was an explosion waiting to happen, and he told Lenore that he would not go back inside it. She nodded again, and replied, "That's sensible, certainly. If you don't mind staying *near* the house, for the night, though, let's do this: I'll get you some clothes to wear that aren't soaked in oil...and you can get cleaned up in the stream while I arrange a little camp here, outside. We can make a fire, so it won't be so cold, and I'll get some bedding. It won't rain until tomorrow, I suspect, so we can have a nice night out under the stars tonight...or clouds, as the case may be."

John had enough of sleeping outdoors when he was in the

militia, but he agreed anyway because he saw how excited Lenore was getting about the idea. She seemed grateful for his agreement, and hurried into the house to gather supplies. John reiterated to her that it was madness to willingly enter such a dangerous place, yet she still went in despite his objections. After a few minutes, she came out with the same bath basket he had used previously, and also some clean clothes.

This was yet another round of giant pants, a brightly-colored robe-tie to be used as a belt, and a flowing, white dress shirt that could easily fit the both of them at once. John did not disparage any of it. His current set of clothing was soaked with kerosene, slashed to shreds in places, and streaked with dirt, so he accepted the ill-fitting clothes without complaint. While he went to the stream to bathe, Lenore entered the house several times, each time emerging with bedding or blankets or cooking utensils or wood to make a campfire. Though she was nearby and could see him bathing, Lenore made no effort to tease John, as she was fully engaged in the task of building a livable outdoor space where they could prepare some food and sleep that evening. For his part, John was not bothered by having her nearby while he bathed, either.

When he came up from the stream wearing the baggy clothes, Lenore had finished building the fire in the middle of the yard, near two mismatched chairs and two mattresses with bedding stacked on top. Lenore sliced up Cartwright's offering of potatoes and, when the fire was burning well enough, began cooking them in a pan over the flames. John could smell the mint that she had mixed in, and thought to himself that this might be the first meal at Everbridge Manor that actually tasted good.

"Don't get your hopes up about the potatoes, John," Lenore cautioned. "I do what I can, but the results are seldom satisfactory, as you know."

"I understand. It's probably hard to plan a meal when you never have the right ingredients."

"Amen!" she said with a chuckle. "Can we talk, while I make the food? Nothing of real import, mind you, but I think some conversation would be very pleasant. I enjoy just being with you."

John nodded and replied, "And I, you, Lenore." He thought of what they could talk about, and said, "Maybe you could tell me something of *your* life...something you're allowed to reveal, of course. Is there some topic that doesn't violate these hidden rules that constraint your speech? If it is not too disturbing for you, can you tell me how it is, for example, that you came to be accused of being a witch, when you are clearly no such thing?"

Her face brightened, and she nodded. "Yes, I *can* tell you that." The fire crackled, its embers popping and cascading in tiny arcs above the logs as Lenore worked the pan. "When I first came to River's Edge, having gained employment as a new teacher at the school, I quickly found myself in unpleasant circumstances. Teaching was fine—great, even—the children were such a joy." Lenore smiled wistfully, recalling her students for a moment with fondness.

John didn't speak, considering the rarity of any full conversation between them, and not wanting to spoil it.

Lenore scraped the potatoes onto two small plates and continued talking. "There was the problem, though, of the headmaster of the school. For some reason, he felt that it was his privilege to take liberties with the women in his employ, and so, I regularly had to fend off his unwanted advances. He was a lonely, bald, petty little man who just would not keep himself to himself. Thankfully, I was lucky and strong enough, at that point, to get him to desist, while still keeping my new job."

The potatoes, which had smelled so delicious while being cooked, were nearly tasteless. They could easily have been parsnips rather than potatoes, or the paste that little children use to glue projects together in school. John didn't say anything about it, though, instead noting, "That sounds like a terrible situation, but it doesn't explain the allegations of witchcraft."

"Doesn't it, though?" Lenore picked at her potatoes, apparently as unimpressed as John as to their quality. "Well, let me clarify the connection for you. I make my own candles and herbal remedies. I know which berries will hurt you, and which will nourish you if they're all you can find. When there are game animals around, I set traps, clean the kills, and dry my own meat. I've always done those things; it is how I was raised."

She frowned, swallowing a bite of flavorless potato with visible effort. "I can cook, too, though you probably don't believe it from these bland results, do you?" She ruefully brushed the rest of her meal into the fire, continuing, "At times during the school year, I passed all of those skills—survival skills—on to the children. Learning can't be all reading and writing and mathematics, especially around here. This is rugged country, John, and boys and girls should be able to take care of themselves, no matter what happens."

She looked over toward the darkened manor, where the windows flickered orange in the firelight. "My life here at Everbridge Manor is a testament to that, now that I think of it. Anyway, in class one day, we made a remedy for restlessness—insomnia—that one of the students called a 'potion.' The class had a good laugh...excepting the sullen looks from the nasty headmaster, there were some fun times around the schoolhouse in those days! And on another day that week, the students asked if there was a potion that could make someone fall in love with you, or could make your hair shiny, or kill someone. Foolishly, because they seemed so engaged in the topic, I agreed that those potions *do* exist...in fact, the insomnia remedy can easily kill, if you use more—and darker —mushrooms."

"Ah. Now I believe I can see where this is going," John said.

"Indeed. It didn't take but a single day for the fateful lesson of the death potion to travel from the lips of one of my precious students, to the ears of one of their parents, and then back to the waiting arms of the spiteful headmaster. Of course, he never forgave me for standing up to his nonsense and making him keep his dirty hands off of me. After another day, the whole thing stopped being about a trifling classroom lark during some useful lessons about survival...and became talk of *witchcraft*. Deadly poisons, evil spells, ensnaring the minds of the little ones, stealing their precious life forces, all that sort of thing."

"I thought people stopped believing in witches decades ago," John observed.

"That's true, but people never stopped believing in *accusing* people of being witches when it suits them, don't you agree? In fact, when there are children involved, even the kindest, most level-headed people can be swayed to injustices in their defense. I was fired from the school right away, of course, but most townspeople were not satisfied to let it end there. Our district stopped hanging and burning and drowning witches years ago, too, but even those ancient, terrible punishments surfaced in town, if only in whispers. One day, my only concern was keeping my job and my dignity amidst an uncertain situation with an insensitive employer...but the next day, I truly feared for my life. There was so much anger—and fear—in the air. I quickly made plans to leave River's Edge."

John motioned toward the manor to one side, and the town to the other. "And yet you still live here, right near the town. How did you avoid what was coming?"

"There was a businessman, somewhat new to town himself, who had set up a trading office and a warehouse for various goods. He became very important to the townspeople, in short order, because he organized the tradesmen and their goods, and was able to put buyers and sellers together in new ways. This man took up my cause, and defended me against the rising tide of rage. Ultimately, his motives were no more pure than those of the headmaster, but the commerce this man brokered was extremely important to River's Edge at the time."

She poked the fire and smiled over at John. "And that, I'm afraid, is as far as I can take that story, as frustrating as that must be to hear. The rest will have to come along another time."

"That was the most you've told me about your life since I came here! Why must you—" John discontinued his question mid-stream and changed it to a different one: "How it is that you are able to tell me that story so readily?"

"That story is *part* of our situation here, but it's not particularly *important* to the situation."

"But...on the topic of the gentleman from town who spoke up for you—"

Lenore shook her head and interrupted, saying quietly, "That man was no gentleman."

John continued, "Fair enough. But I believe I have seen his portrait at the top of the stairs." Lenore neither agreed, nor disagreed, though she did accidentally drop a fork near John while he continued, "At least tell me this..." John kneeled to pick up the fork, and handed it up to her. "Are you...married?" Instead of taking the fork, though, Lenore took his hand in both of hers and replied, with an exaggerated giggle, "Why, be still my heart! A handsome man is on one knee before me, asking me about marriage! What shall I do?"

When he realized that he *was* kneeling before her in just such a position, he drew his hand away and stood up abruptly. "What? No. That wasn't exactly...that's not what I'm asking." Lenore just laughed, and after a few moments, John gave in and joined her.

"I know that's not what you're asking, John, and I even know *why* 'are you married' is a question you have. I don't mind it. I just like to have some fun when you're poking around for your answers. It's so easy to get you flustered; I can't resist sometimes."

In the downstairs parlor window, the curtains moved, and John wondered if they could lessen their encounters with evil spirits by staying out here in the yard. Of course, he had encountered the strange, old innkeeper out here that one time, so it didn't seem likely that camping outdoors would make any difference to whatever hauntings might occur. Indeed, Lenore noticed him looking at the movement of the curtains, and said quietly, "Don't think that staying outside will make them leave us alone, John."

Lenore put two new logs into the fire and began setting up the bedding on the mattresses, saying, "We should probably turn in for the night."

The mattresses were right next to each other, with the fire at their feet. After they settled in, and when both John and Lenore were lying on their backs, facing the unsettled night sky, she said, "To answer your real question, John, I have never been legally married."

He nodded, but also thought about Kitty and Rooster, and Rooster's odd clarification that they had a 'common law' marriage. "You said 'legally' like it is one of your clever evasions, Lenore. Is there some *other* type of marriage, one that is not legal?"

"I guess two people, in the very best of times, can just decide to be wed to one another, without any license or paperwork. Maybe it's illegal *somewhere*, but why should the laws of man get in the way of love?"

"Have you ever been married *illegally*, Lenore?"

John could hear the amusement in her voice as she said, "Oh, yes. Lots of times."

John closed his eyes, listening to the fire crackle and the

stream lap gently against the shore nearby. Lenore said, "Now, go to sleep, my love."

AFTER A RESTLESS NIGHT of bad dreams, John woke before Lenore did. He quietly put another log on the fire, and watched her sleeping near him for a few moments. She was restless and unhappy in what looked like her own intense nightmares. If her dreams were as vivid as his, she was re-living some painful moment from the past. The sun, almost invisible behind the ever-present, obscuring screen of clouds, began to rise, providing just a small amount of light to their courtyard campground. Lenore's face was somehow familiar to him, as if he had met her *before* all of this, or as if she resembled someone else he already knew.

He could not remember it, though, so, taking care not to wake Lenore, John rose to use the nearby outhouse. He brought a small candle along, lit from the fire, for the inside of the outhouse was always very dark. While attending to his business, he remembered a day when he and Kitty were eight or nine years old, where his sister had used a kitchen knife to carve her name in the wood slats behind the outhouse. Knowing that damage to the house or the grounds was something their Aunt would not tolerate, John had told his sister not to do it...but then she made it even worse by carving *his* name there, too! Kitty never missed a chance to get John in trouble, enjoying it most if she could somehow escape a reprimand for her own works, while sticking John with the punishment. There had been a distinct, rounded knot in the wood, shaped like an apple, and Kitty has used that blackened knot as the "O" in JOHN. At the time, he had been afraid they would both get in trouble, but thankfully nothing had ever come of it. Their Aunt Agnes *did* use the outhouse, of course, but she seldom wandered beyond her set path outside, preferring instead to remain indoors most of the time.

Interested in seeing how twenty years of passed time had affected Kitty's wayward scratchings, John went behind the outhouse to look. He was surprised to see that their names were no longer etched back there. He immediately thought that someone had repaired the damage, but then noticed that familiar, apple-shaped knot. Though once used as a deformed letter "O," it was now unadorned, with no damage visible anywhere near it. Kitty had been rough about her work; there would be no fixing it while also keeping that knot intact. If anything, John noticed, the whole outhouse looked *newer* than it had ever looked when he had lived here. Yet there it was, the same distinct, undamaged knot in the same slat.

It didn't make any sense, but that was no different than many other things since John had returned to the manor. Instead of just noting how odd this was and stumbling cluelessly on to the next odd thing, John thought that it was long past time to take stock of what he thought was going on at Everbridge Manor. Lenore wasn't going to help him, obviously, but regrouping and considering some solutions to the many mysteries around here could keep him from getting hurt or killed.

Though he could remember nothing of the circumstances of her death, John *did* know that his mother had passed away long ago. Growing up at the Manor with an aunt from his father's side of the family, it was always clear to John and Kitty that neither of them had any living relatives left besides Aunt Agnes herself. So the beckoning woman he had seen yesterday —the woman he now knew looked just like his mother, wearing the very same ragged clothes she had been wearing on their hasty journey from Junction City—was a dead person. It was some kind of spirit, or ghost, or manifestation; there was no other way to look at it. This made him accept something he had been avoiding thinking about thus far: his step-sister Kitty had also appeared to him a few times, in exactly the same manner as his mother. Therefore, Kitty was also a spirit, and was also dead. It hurt his heart to acknowledge it, but there it was. John didn't believe in ghosts, yet he had no choice but to accept what his own eyes had shown him.

Standing behind the outhouse, looking down at the place where some children's names were *not carved*, John next thought about the environment he was in. Normally, the weather in this district was cold and clear, with occasional rain or snow, but the sky here at the manor was continually, unnaturally dark. On the one occasion it cleared up, the rapid transitions were nothing short of impossible. There had been a giant, twisting, blue funnel behind the house as well, with unbelievable, eye-adorned tendrils snaking out through the soil...and the whole, giant mass of it had blasted out of sight into the ground in a most unnatural way. Rivers did not usually flow in two different directions.

John felt like he was being watched, and he looked up to see the little boy inside the manor, observing him. The child wore a hateful expression and had tucked himself inside the curtains near the hallway clock, where he stared out at John. John walked closer to the window, observing the boy as he did so. "Who are you, boy? Why do you hate me so?"

Someone with no affinity for scissors had cut the boy's straight black hair, John noticed, as the boy continued sneering at him. His messy hair had been sheared at an unfortunate angle across his forehead. The boy's clothes were what John would call "fancy clothes," but they had suffered terribly since being donned. First, the boy himself had probably put on the clothes, as the shirt buttons were misaligned. Second, the boy had probably played in them for some time, tearing the shoulder of the shirt and generally dirtying up the whole affair.

As John came close to the window, the boy pressed both of

his hands to the sides of his own head and elaborately pretended to squish them together. As he pantomimed this action, he slowly stuck out his tongue, screwed up his eyes, and tilted his head toward his shrugging shoulders. A moment later, he withdrew from inside the curtain, out of sight.

This strange occurrence just made John more perplexed, as he walked away from the window and back toward the camp. *Everything* around the manor was so implausible, so artificial, it was hard to know what to think. The only thing that seemed *real* here was Lenore herself. Though she suspiciously dodged all attempts to glean information from her, she at least stayed put when you looked away from her, and she didn't attack him or try to scare him as the others had. She had in fact *saved* him from harm on several occasions. Additionally, John admitted to himself that he was also starting to have feelings for her, despite her evasions; he was not willing to entertain the idea that she was a spirit like the strange boy in the window, and so dismissed it entirely.

Yes, he believed that he and Lenore were *real*—what else could they be? But, as unreasonable as it might seem, it was *just possible* that the rest of this was...not real. He didn't know what "not real" was, in this case, but many facts were apparent to support that type of conclusion. Of course, another conclusion was that he had gone completely insane. Crazy people saw crazy things all the time; that thought was comforting because it didn't make *ghosts* into a real thing. Insanity fit the facts nicely, too, he knew, and it might be less troubling when all was said and done. "Not real" was some unstable ground all of its own.

As he walked back to where Lenore was sleeping, John considered the newness of the outhouse, its apple-shaped knot, and the missing names. There *was* a time, he thought, when that outhouse was newer, when its boards were unscarred by nine-year-old Kitty's gleeful defacements.

That time was *before* Kitty had carved their names into the boards. If John was going to believe that "not real" was a possibility, he would also have to believe that "before" was a possibility, too.

Or maybe he was just crazy. Given the alternatives, that would be grand.

WHEN LENORE DREAMED, it was the same as when John dreamed: an endless repeat of past tragedies, and the lead-up to them. She had no control of her thoughts, or her actions. Each dream was a *reliving*, exactly like being awake and present and experiencing those earlier events for the very first time.

In this part, she was upstairs at the manor sitting before her tall mirror, examining a cut that traced the line of her left eyebrow, and feeling the joint of her jaw to determine how much pain there was going to be in opening her mouth for the next few days. In the wake of yet another argument, yet another attack, she was considering her options. She needed to get away from her husband before he beat her to death.

Her husband's given name was Bertram, but a combination of self-loathing and self-aggrandizement made him demand that everyone call him "The Master." He was an angry, scheming, defensive tyrant, and had never been otherwise for the entire time she knew him. Normally, such a piggish man would not have warranted a sliver of consideration from Lenore, but a dire circumstance presented itself to him that allowed him to claim Lenore for his own, with her willing cooperation. When Lenore was twenty-four years old, she was a schoolteacher in River's Edge, where The Master plied his trade as a conduit for goods and services in the district.

After a ludicrous scandal at the schoolhouse, Lenore lost her job, but rumors persisted that harsher penalties would need to be paid. It was here that The Master stepped in, manufacturing a romantic relationship between himself and Lenore through sheer force of will, and he demanded that the townspeople stand down. He did it to prove to them that he *could*...to make it clear that they needed *him* more than they needed their vengeance. He also did it because he *wanted* Lenore, though prior to her troubles, they had hardly exchanged five words during the whole time she lived in town. He did it because it gave him an opportunity to *own* Lenore, with no real chance that she could ever get away.

It became immediately clear to Lenore that finding herself under the control of The Master was a huge mistake. She should have run away from the town instead of accepting his help; with their children out of danger, and the ridiculousness of the accusations, the townspeople probably wouldn't have pursued her vigorously at all.

The Master controlled his appetites and his anger in exactly equal measure, which was to say that he did not control them at all. He demanded sexual favors from her on the very first evening after he got the townspeople to back off, and regularly thereafter. These events were unpleasant for all participants except The Master himself, always including far more violence than sexuality. Lenore usually had the bruises from the previous encounter when the next began, which is just how he liked it.

Lenore and The Master were married within two weeks of the scandal, and she was instructed to stay at Everbridge Manor and not visit the town at all. It all seemed to her like one of those pixie tales where the princess is locked in a tower in the service of some foul beast, with no means of escape whatsoever. Within two months of her imprisonment, she became pregnant, which enraged The Master even further, especially as she grew with child; he tried to beat the baby out of her on more than one occasion. Miraculously, her daughter arrived, seemingly unharmed, which brought Lenore a measure of joy in her now-darkened world.

The Master employed a maid, whose real name was Clara, but whom he always just called "Matron." When the baby came, he arranged for the matron to work and stay full-time at the manor. She was a stout, cheerless woman, prone to hot flashes and redness of the face, but nonetheless a competent cook and a discrete servant. The matron—Clara—was not a young woman, and was always winded after a small amount of work or strife; Lenore frequently worried about the state of the plump woman's heart. And though the matron knew of the beatings that Lenore regularly endured, she never intervened. She herself had never been struck by The Master, but she had seen enough to know that there was no ruling it out. His anger was a towering thing indeed.

Though having a beautiful baby of her own warmed her heart, over the years, the overall situation seemed more and more hopeless to Lenore. She began thinking, quite seriously, of throwing herself from the roof of the manor, ending both her pain and her life at the same time. She imagined one instant of red pain, followed by an eternity of black silence. She longed to do it, too, but there was one thing that stood in the way of that alternate means of escape. Jumping from the roof would leave Lenore's daughter entirely under her husband's control, with no loving mother to keep her safe from his anger. Lenore had no money of her own, no real power at all. Her husband had even told her that the manor itself would not be hers should he die; his will explicitly gave everything to their daughter, not to Lenore, and there were written instructions to evict Lenore should any harm come to The Master.

Lenore's daughter was now five years old, and today, after the girl spilled some milk at the afternoon meal table, The Master had slapped the girl for the first time. Lenore had objected, which earned her a trio of cracks of her own, one of which opened the cut above her eye. The Master had gone back to work, leaving Lenore to attend to her shocked and saddened and crying daughter—with the nervous matron's help—for the rest of the afternoon.

It was not hard to see that her daughter was going to become a second target for her husband's bottomless rage, and that could not be allowed to start. And so, Lenore sat at the mirror and considered her injuries and her options. She was thirty years old, with no resources and no recourses, but still, she gave serious thought to just taking her daughter and fleeing. Her husband, however, was powerful and ruthless; if his wife and daughter ran away one day, he would stop at nothing to find them. He would resurrect the old rumors, as he often threatened to do, and would use them to enlist the whole world in finding the fugitives.

There was knock downstairs, on the front door, and Lenore heard the matron go to answer it. A few moments later, there came some raised voices, including the matron's, and Lenore heard her daughter coming up the stairs.

The little girl came in the bedroom, saying, "Momma, there's a woman at the door...with a boy." Lenore took a moment to look over her daughter, five years old and so small and lovely. She looked so much like her mother that their relation could not be mistaken.

Lenore tried to manage a smile. "All right, Kitty," she said. "I'll be down in a moment."

Lenore was still sleeping when John returned from the outhouse. He lay down on his bed and again watched her as she twitched in her restless sleep, his mind open to new possibilities of what might be "real" or "not real." As he looked closely at her beautiful face, framed with familiar, long black hair, she opened her hazel eyes. He recognized those eyes as bearing a striking resemblance to someone else in his life... someone who, at last check, was about the same age as he was, just then. She and John were both thirty years old. Lenore, impossibly, was *also* thirty years old, just then. It was incredible, but it was right. It was the first aspect of *unreality* that John chose to simply accept, and this terrified him. In his mind, he conjured up a recollection of the large kerosene jar in the basement that had, above it, a painting of a black-haired woman holding a swaddled child.

Lenore smiled kindly at him as she awoke, but then noticed the concern on his face. She sat up. "John? What wrong?"

"Are you, or were you, someone's wife?"

She narrowed her eyebrows. "Why, yes, but—"

A resonant hum started to rise from the direction of the manor as John asked, "Are you someone's mother?"

She closed and opened her eyes, trying to wake up completely. "Do we really need to do this right now? Maybe you could keep your conclusions to yourself for a bit longer."

The hum rose. The ground began to tremble, and the wooden spoon that Lenore had used for the previous night's meal rattled in the unwashed pan. John ignored all of that. "No. Answer my question."

Lenore looked anxiously over toward the manor as a peculiar wind built around them. "But we'll lose the front door. Please."

"I don't know what that means, but I won't let you evade me on this. I demand an answer to my question."

"Yes. I am someone's mother. What is it that's gotten you into this state, John? The chains and chimes of the hallway clock?" She looked over toward the outhouse and nodded. "Oh, the knot-hole?"

It made no sense to John, but he said what he now knew. "You're Kitty's mother."

She nodded, slowly, and whispered, "Yes."

The rumble immediately pitched to a deafening roar, and then a gigantic crash of smashing glass came from inside the manor, and the whole front door blew outward in a massive gust of oily air. Kerosene fumes reached them all the way in the yard, burning the soft tissue inside John's nose as he turned his face away. The front door, askew and attached by one twisted hinge, knocked around on the porch in the flurry.

They were silent for a minute as the vibrations in the air and the ground slowed and eventually stopped. John thought about the giant kerosene jars in the basement, believing that one of them had just exploded...by some inexplicable force of strange magic. Out loud, he said, "It was the jar—the *vessel*, to use your term from the other day—that had the painting of you with the baby."

Lenore lay down on her back on the mattress, saying, "I call that one the vessel of motherhood, for what it's worth." She stared at the sky. It began to rain, lightly.

"Your resemblance to her is unmistakable," John said, also laying back down, but facing Lenore instead of the sky. With the rain starting, he thought that they would need to move the bedding to the porch if they cared for it to stay dry. "I'm surprised I didn't put it together before."

Lenore said, "Just in case you get any ideas on the topic, I should clarify: you and I are *not* related, in any way."

John said, "Good to know."

Just on the other side of Lenore, the old woman Innkeeper sat up, whisking into view as if she had been sleeping there the whole time. Her eyes were huge and black and ancient, and her mouth was contorted in a grimace of hate made all the more terrifying by its lack of most of her teeth. She suddenly clambered over Lenore, shrieking, dragging her dark scarf and heavy cloak behind her, coming at John's face with gnarled fingers, jagged fingernails approaching his eyes. This enraged old woman was on top of him before he knew it, and John flailed his arms up and around trying to fend her off. One of her nails raked across his ear, and he felt it tear through the skin.

Lenore moved to help, but in the next moment, the little boy also came up from her other side, as if he, too had just been sleeping there, next to the old woman. Like the Innkeeper, he was yelling—screaming out angry nonsense cries—and within a few seconds, he was over Lenore and was pounding John on the head with his little fists, was kicking at him in the side.

Lenore was there, too, pushing the boy in one direction and the old woman in the other. For ten seconds, there were eight arms and eight legs all flying and flailing, with four people scuffling on the same, single mattress in a big pile. Neither of his attackers weighed very much, though, so John was able to throw them off and roll away from the bed, away from the fire, in the direction of the house.

When he finished his roll and scrambled to his feet, neither the little boy nor the old woman was visible anywhere. John just stood there, breathing heavily, holding his ear, as he looked down on Lenore. At first, she was tangled up in his blankets, but then she also gained her feet. After she caught her breath, she started to drag the mattresses and bedding over to the porch where they could stay dry during the day's rain.

After she came back from dragging the second one, she said, "Well, such an eventful morning! It looks like it's really going to rain today. Shall we just go inside, sit by the fire, and do some reading?" John didn't answer. Lenore said, "I can try to do something with those coconuts."

John was having none of her levity, nor was he planning to fall for the "tasty food" trick another time. He was instead thinking of the two basement kerosene jars with their smoky, scary imagery of some cataclysm or other, most likely in River's Edge. He was sure that those two jars were as yet unbroken.

Was he intended to solve some collection of mysteries, smashing all of the jars through the force of his discoveries, to find a way out of this place? Lenore moved her head back and forth slowly while holding his gaze, as if reading his mind and providing her own form of answer.

"No," he said firmly. "I think we should go into town. I told Cartwright I would see to his paid commission, and I intend to do that."

She replied, "As you wish, John." Without saying anything else, she walked around on both sides of the house, apparently looking for something. When she spotted it, she said, "Ah, there you are," and walked out of sight for a moment, before returning with John's horse.

Lenore lead His Majesty over to them, and nodded toward the Everbridge. She apparently didn't mean to ride the horse, only to bring it along. She asked, "Shall we go?"

THE LIGHT RAIN continued as Lenore and John made their way across the Everbridge. The river ran below them, eventually winding its way to River's Edge. The road to the right lead to Junction city, and the one to the left to River's Edge. John knew it was only a short walk to town, perhaps ten minutes. Lenore took John's hand in hers, and he did not complain about it as they turned left and proceeded amiably together toward town. They walked His Majesty alongside them, eventually coming upon some small cottages on the right side of the road, facing out to the river.

John went up to one of the houses and knocked on the door, while Lenore waited at the road with the horse. No one answered the door, despite several concerted attempts to raise the residents inside. John tried the front door to see if it was locked, and found that it was not. He went inside, and after a few moments Lenore joined him.

The cottage was a simple, one-room affair, with a sleeping space off to one side, some bookshelves containing old books, and a kitchen area with a round table. There was a small vase on the table, with a single daisy sticking out of it. The whole house felt silent, almost airless.

John stepped over to the daisy and touched it with his finger. At once, the whole flower and its stem crumbled into white dust, which drifted to the tabletop in an excruciatingly slow fashion. John said, "Hmm," while Lenore said nothing.

It was clear to John that nobody had lived here for a very long time.

John knocked the vase over on purpose, not breaking it, but listening to the sound it made when it struck the wooden table-top. As John expected, the sound was...muted. He picked up the vase and examined it: a simple, glass vase.

Holding the vase, John said, "This house reminds me of a creepy diorama I saw once at the Junction City fair. So still and silent, as if *waiting* for something to happen. I feel like I could drop this, and it would just hang in the air."

After a moment, Lenore replied, "Don't worry, things still fall to the ground here, John. We *do* have gravity near the manor, and also here in town."

To test this, he dropped the vase, which smashed on the floor with little or no sound. He looked at Lenore, as if waiting for her to say something.

She gave no reaction. "What is it?"

"I guess I was expecting you to say not to make a mess. You *were* a schoolteacher, after all, as well as a mother?"

"Yes on both, as you know...but you can do what you want here. This isn't my house."

"Would you say that Everbridge Manor *is* your house?"

They left the small cottage as Lenore replied, smiling, "Back to the questions again. Always the investigator."

When they stepped outside, the clouds seemed much darker, sending larger raindrops falling to the road. Lenore looked up at the sky and said, "This rain looks a lot heavier...try not to get a raindrop in your eye."

At this, John looked up at the sky, and right at that moment, a fat raindrop fell and landed directly in his left eye. He exclaimed in surprise, sputtering and shaking his head and brushing the water away. "Ah, what? What are the...what are the chances of *that*?"

Lenore giggled. "About one in five, I would say."

"That's incredibly specific. *What* is going on? What are you playing at, madam?"

She just shrugged. "Whenever things get too serious, John, I feel like we should have a laugh. And don't go back to calling me 'madam, 'or I shall have to call you..."

Finally catching on, John shook his head, grinning. "No... don't. Really."

"Yes, yes," Lenore replied, "I shall call you, 'Raindrop'!" It was all pure silliness, but there was a strange tension growing in the still air as they moved toward town, and both of them had a wary, guarded laugh.

They continued to another house, a few minutes on, and repeated the process John had undertaken in the first one: knock, enter, examine, disturb something, and leave. To John, everything about these cottages beside the road seemed static, artificial, almost like scenes viewed through gauze.

They were still a few minutes from town when Lenore said, "What was that you said about the Junction City fair? I may know something of the diorama you were describing."

"We visited it once, when I was about ten...my sister and me, and my aunt," John said. "One of the artisans was showing off mechanical toys and clever clockworks, and Kitty found a big, old, mechanical diorama in one of his back stalls. A 'story table,' I remember someone calling it. I believe the artisan's father had made it, years before...but even though it was probably magnificent at one time, it was broken and covered up with a tarp. Kitty pulled the cover off and showed it to me."

"Ah, that's a machine that I saw when I was a girl, too," Lenore said, "when it was working in its full glory. So intricate, with all sorts of movement and colorful art and clever clock-work animation! It *was* just a bit frightening for children to see, now that I think about it. But please tell me more; I enjoy hearing about you and Kitty, from those earlier times."

They could see the town of River's Edge up ahead, and now they could also smell the ever-present smoke. "When I saw it," John continued, "it was just a round table with five or six scenes: a scary forest, a parlor, a bedroom, a dark cave with spotted mushrooms. There were slots where characters and things were supposed to pop up, or rise up, I guess...but nothing was there. The whole contraption was completely still, frozen, like these houses here. I got up really close to it, and what was most scary to me was the idea that something would pop out of one of those slots right while I was staring. Kitty even tried to frighten me by grabbing my arm and yelling, 'Boo!'"

"Since you saw it in its prime," John continued, "maybe you can tell me what it was supposed to be about. What *was* it, besides a way to unsettle nosy children who poked around in the back where they weren't allowed?"

"Most of it was the pixie tale of Lindy Crimson Cloak," Lenore said. "You know the one, where she gets eaten at the end, by the forest beast wearing her aunt's robes?"

John nodded, wrinkling his nose against the bitter smell of smoke, as Lenore continued, "Well, the old artisan would wind the machine up, and for the next ten minutes, the table would rotate and Lindy would progress from wedge to wedge, entering each different scene while it sort of...came alive. She got set upon by the black wolves in the forest, all teeth and mangy fur. And then she encountered the three house-grizzlies from that other story. That scene was set in the grizzlies' crooked bedroom where their beds tilted too much, not enough, and just enough. Those grizzlies loomed up over her on all sides, again with the teeth and the claws!" She motioned with her hands, mimicking claws coming together from the sides to rend poor Lindy. "And then she would appear in the next scene, on her cushion in the parlor with her oatmeal, and this huge orange and black spider would spring out from a cabinet!"

John sighed as they entered the town proper, now moving down the long, main street. No fire had affected the structures on the first part of the street: a blacksmith, the town municipal office, and the police station. "There *was* something orange sticking out of one of the slots!" he continued. "I bet that was the clockwork spider! Good thing it didn't pop out while I was peeking!" John tried to stay in the mood of their lighthearted conversation, but an unsettling dread had started to build in him. "I remember Kitty was affected by the whole thing, too, saying that the scenes reminded her of her own life. All those scary, frozen tableaus. I couldn't understand her saying that... her life was mostly the same as mine, with the three of us in the manor, and there wasn't much 'scary' anything around then. But I soon learned Kitty had a skewed way of perceiving things."

The buildings on both sides of the main street were intact, though they all looked as lifeless and inert as the cottages they had passed. There were no other people to be seen. Up ahead on the left, one of the buildings was smoldering and emitting a giant pillar of black smoke. John's lips pressed together in concern.

Lenore agreed with what John had said about Kitty. "Poor

thing; all of that breaks my heart. But I'll tell you this: the thing about the diorama that disturbed *me* the most was that it just went around and around. Lindy popped up in each wedge, got set upon by monsters and beasts, and then popped up in the next one, over and over. I remember wishing there was some kind of final scene where she could just get a good night's sleep or could enjoy a cup of tea by the fire without any fiendish clockwork slots disgorging horrors at her."

They arrived at the source of one of the two smoky pillars in the town: a business office just across from the old general store. There was a warehouse building attached to the business office, and it appeared that both of those structures had burned up in the last few hours. Some walls were partially intact, so the shape of the two areas was still delineated, but neither room had any roof left to speak of. There would be no repair against this tremendous damage. All of the remaining timbers were hot and glowing with embers; the entire building radiated an intense heat. John could barely see beyond the smoke into the office...a dark, burned-out wreck, its floor covered in ash and blackened wood fragments. Looking toward this scene made his heart race. Raindrops sizzled on the wreckage. He gritted his teeth as his stomach took one great lurch. The stench of burning flesh blew out of the building before him. Sweat broke out on his brow.

John had been here before.

"And speaking of horrors," Lenore said. "Here we are."

JOHN PEERED into the smoke-filled office, smelling the burned bodies and forcing himself not to gag. "Now this...*this*..." he began, clenching both fists and taking a moment to steady himself. "This feels *real*."

Lenore was at his side, handing him a handkerchief to put

up over his mouth against the smoke, and gently wrapping one of her arms into his. "Yes, my love. This *is* real. Beyond this threshold, your heart, and your stomach, must become steel."

He didn't move. "People died here. And I have been here myself; I can feel it. A part of me fears what I'll find out about myself if we enter."

Lenore nodded, and squeezed his arm in an attempt to comfort him. "It is a grizzly business, but perhaps you can focus on your role as a police investigator, trying objectively to get to the bottom of a terrible crime."

She gently pulled his arm, and moved them forward, toward what was previously the front door of the office. John shook his head. "There aren't very many suspects, Lenore. I still have large gaps in my memory, and if someone killed these people, I fear that it might have been *me*. A part of me remembers standing right here, looking in at this scene." He pointed to the spot where he was currently standing, right in the center of the room's former doorway.

Lenore nodded, again guiding him forward. "Well, if it can help you through this day, through the tragic scene before us, let me tell you this, my love: You didn't kill these people. You are no more of a murderer than I am."

They covered their noses with the handkerchiefs and entered the hazy business office, where, despite the smoke, every detail appeared to John with a hyper-realistic cast. This was the *opposite* of the cottages out there; nothing here would crumble away inconsequentially at his touch. He felt that everything here was meant to *last* and be held up to his scrutiny. There was a huge, burned-out mahogany desk in the center of the room, behind which was a sizeable metal and wooden chair, also partially burned. Atop the remains of the chair, sitting at the remains of the desk, was a large man's smoldering corpse. His body was a riot of blackness, with red flesh showing through the char in some places. Despite a fire that was hot enough to burn away all evidence of hair and clothing, the man still retained some semblance of his positioning when he died. Before his death, this individual had been very large and round indeed. His head and shoulders were slumped down on the desk, atop one massive arm and a few stacks of partially burned papers; the man's right hand was lifted up, pressing against some pain or injury on his neck on that side.

John and Lenore stood on the front side of the desk, saying nothing while looking down at the large, dead man opposite them.

At a normal crime scene, John's mind would be working through the possibilities of how the offence occurred, who the victims were, but he had not yet engaged that thought process. Instead, he was experiencing an inexplicable, deep-seated fear, similar in its way to the one he had sometimes felt when passing by the basement stairwell, back at the manor, yet so much worse. There was something here that wanted to reduce John to being just a scared little boy. Perhaps it was related to this big man when he was alive, or in his manner of death. John didn't know; he could not focus on that. Instead, he felt a power in this room that threatened to jar loose a terrible, buried secret that he would not want to view. He was trying to bring that ancient terror under control, and he found that having Lenore hold his arm tightly was part of doing that. He continued to scan across the atrocities of the room, as yet numb to its mysteries.

To the right of the desk, near the partial wall that once separated the office from the warehouse, a woman's body lay on the ground. Like the man, there were no clothes or hair to be seen, the fire having burned all of that away prior to burning away much of her remains. Unlike the man, who had apparently been holding a hand over some neck wound when he died, with no weapon visible, the woman's cause of death was still sticking out of her eye-socket: a thin letter opener, its handle blackened from the spilled blood that had burned all over its surface. There were two smashed kerosene lanterns in this area, their fuel perhaps having contributed to the original fire. Looking at this unrecognizable woman made John incredibly sad, not just in the manner of her death, but in some other subconscious way that he dared not name, or even acknowledge in his own head.

Lenore slowly lead John around on the other side of the desk, behind the large man, where they approached the woman's corpse from the opposite direction. On John's left, where the wall between the office and the warehouse once stood, John noted evidence of a large explosion. Something had been on the warehouse side of the wall, he thought, and when that something exploded, it blasted through the wall into the office, while also devastating the warehouse room beyond. John observed that the explosion had *not* killed the man or woman, or at least he did not think it had done so. Perhaps they were dead, or dying, before the explosion occurred.

Shards of glass and shreds of thin metal streaked out from the center of the detonation; John could see twisted lids of jelly jars—normal sized ones—as well as fragments of their thick glass all around. The shreds of metal came from cans of some type of organic content, such as some fruits or vegetables, though none of the paper labels were left to read.

Lenore gently tugged John closer to that giant hole leading to the warehouse, where the third and final body was visible through what was once the wall. A man in the warehouse had been viciously shredded in whatever explosion had occurred, and his dead body had then burned up afterward when the rest of these two rooms went up in flames. The dead warehouse man brought up no particular feelings in John, besides the compassion he felt when anyone's life was ended with sudden violence...certainly he felt nothing that rivalled his reactions of fear of the big man and of sadness for the dead woman.

John patted Lenore's helping hand, withdrew her arm, and stepped into the warehouse, saying, "I'm going to have a closer look." Lenore responded by saying, "Of course," and she stepped back behind the chair with the large, dead man in it. While John walked through the remains of the warehouse, Lenore watched him, a look of resigned sadness on her face.

The far side of the warehouse had burned down from the fire as well, but it was not as damaged as the part close to the source of the explosion. Over on that side, John found some relatively intact, though crushed and empty, tin cans, confirming that the organic matter was indeed some fruit...in this case, sliced peaches. Behind a tall, twisted metal shelf, he also found one of the glass jelly-jars, intact, with its lid still in place. It was a normal-sized version of the jelly-jars in Lenore's basement. It was filled, in fact, with yellowish liquid that John knew, with certainty, was kerosene. The metal shelf had fallen atop it in such a way that it had been protected from the burning building, though there was nothing to say that it would not explode now. John used the sleeve of his giant, flowing white shirt to grab the jar, which he walked outside of the warehouse by stepping over the crumbled far wall. He set the kerosene down out there, where it would not explode and do harm to him or Lenore.

His investigative instincts were becoming activated, and he went back over to have a look around the office. Of course, there were no telltale footprints or other easy clues to help him solve the crime, but he came up with a few plausible theories. The least-likely was that the man and the woman had killed each other somehow, with the letter opener ending up in the woman's face...the altercation somehow also dislodging and igniting the kerosene lanterns. The blazing lanterns had then burned through the thin plywood wall to the warehouse, reaching a strange, nearby stack of glass kerosene jars and peaches in tin cans, which exploded and killed the man working there. John had never known kerosene to be stored in these types of jars, but it was believable that somehow it had happened here. The more-likely theory was that someone else, either the warehouse-man or someone not currently in evidence, had killed the man and then the woman, somehow igniting the lamp-based explosion sequence before dying in the warehouse, if the killer had been the warehouse man, or otherwise, fleeing the scene.

John unconsciously avoided speculation about the identities of the victims. There was no need, at this time, to look too closely toward what his subconscious told him would likely be a painful conclusion.

Lenore was standing nearby, still covering her nose with the handkerchief, saying nothing as she watched him look around. John briefly perused through the papers on the desk, finding nothing of interest. He scanned around the other parts of the office, also without finding any additional clues.

Eventually, John felt that there was nothing more he could learn here. He said, "All right. I've seen what there is to see. It's time to bury these poor people."

Lenore actually laughed. "Really? No, John, that's not necessary."

"It's not right to leave these bodies here to rot, Lenore. They deserve a proper burial."

She shook her head slowly and said, "Truly, I understand why you might feel that needs to be done, but burying these three people, that's just a waste of time."

John thought to himself that the witch-fearing townspeople might take further issue with Lenore if they heard that she objected to dead people being buried in a proper grave. He started to ask, "Why?" but stopped himself. There was little point in asking her such questions. He shrugged and started toward the ruined front doorway of the office. "You don't have to assist me if you don't wish to, Lenore. But I'm going to do this."

When he reached the doorway, he again felt that strange feeling of having already been here, and he turned around on the spot and looked back over the scene, trying to discern what the feeling was telling him. But, having cut off all thought processes that would lead to speculation about who these murder victims actually were, he learned nothing new.

Lenore said, "I again recommend *not* doing what you're suggesting, John, but it's not because I'm a witch who wants to stand in the way of respectable burials, for some nefarious reason. But I said I would help you, and I meant it. If your mind is set on this, I *will* help you bury them."

And help him she did. She knew just what supplies would be needed from the darkened general store, and she knew of a spot near the front of the town graveyard—which itself was behind the municipal building—where the ground was soft for easier digging. She hitched a tarp to His Majesty, upon which they carefully loaded the bodies, making the haul to the grave-yard that much simpler. The rain was a factor in that it beat on them as they worked, but it also further softened the dirt they had to move. Lenore dug one grave at the same time as John dug a second, and then they worked together on the last one. It was slow, brutal, dirty work, which continued to levy a heavy emotional toll on John, even as the long hours passed. Their clothes became soiled with the mud of the graves and the blood and burnt flesh of the charred bodies. It took all the way into the late afternoon to complete the three jobs. After they buried all of the corpses and covered them up, they stood before the fresh graves for a few minutes while John tried to think of something to say. A part of him wanted to cry, but John did not let that part get its way.

When no useful words came to John after a time, Lenore spoke up, facing toward the graves and saying sincerely, "May the Maker bless and keep you." This seemed satisfactory to John, who nodded over at her in thanks.

Far down the main street, on the other side of River's Edge, another pillar of smoke rose. It seemed to be coming from the area where the town's inn was, and John assumed that it, too, would bear investigation. By now, he had a fair idea of the type of thing they would see there, something probably even worse than what they saw today in the office. He had endured enough of it for one day, and told Lenore that they would come back the next day to see to the rest. She had no objection.

The rain subsided—though the sky remained gray and overcast, as it always was—as they walked back to the manor, hand-in-hand, silently towing John's horse while nursing their newly-sore muscles.

THEY ARRIVED BACK at Everbridge Manor as the last of the day's light—what little there ever was, the sky being overcast all day —faded. John looked around for a place to hitch his horse, but Lenore said, "There's no need for that." She took the reins from him, dropped them, patted His Majesty on the rump, and gently said, "Go on." His Majesty trotted off toward the spindly trees behind the manor.

The front door of the manor was still hanging by one hinge, and the smell of kerosene was thick in the air near the doorway. Lenore ignored this and went in to get some clean clothes for the both of them and the bathing baskets, while John moved the mattresses and bedding back toward their makeshift fire pit. It took a while for Lenore to emerge with her supplies, and when she did, John noticed that her nose was bleeding. He asked her what had happened inside, and she shook her head while wiping away the blood. "It's nothing, my love. Well, nothing *new*, anyway. I'll be fine."

Lenore then went to retrieve some firewood from indoors, and this time John stood in the dark front doorway to watch after her. She could only carry a few pieces of the heavy, split wood at a time, so John bucked up and walked into the house with her, all the way into the parlor on her second trip, where she silently loaded his arms up with the remaining firewood from a storage cubby near the fireplace. Outside, they started the fire in the pit near the beds, and then went to the bathing hole to clean up after their adventures in the office and the graveyard.

On the shore of the bathing hole, they stripped out of their clothes and carried their respective lumps of soap out into the cool water. There, they silently washed off the mud and soot and blood, watching each other as they did. There was none of the teasing, playful air from their previous shared bath; but instead, there was a warming atmosphere of comfortably-shared intimacy. After a time, they were both done washing off the dirt from their labors, and Lenore smiled over at John in a kind way that made him smile back and want to take her up into his arms right then. He did, moving closer to her and pulling her into a tender embrace, their arms wrapped around each other and squeezing tightly. She pulled him so close against her that he had a little trouble breathing, and he loved it. She tucked her head under the crook of his neck, and they stood there in the water for a long time, each just enjoying the feel of the other's body, pressed so closely together.

Eventually, they began to kiss, as they had done once on the roof after narrowly escaping a plunge to their deaths. This time, their kisses were just as sweet, but there was a heated, sensual aspect to them that surprised and thrilled John as they made their way to the shore, toweled off, and walked merrily to the beds without bothering with their clothes.

They made love by the fire, and John knew without any doubt that it was the best sex that he would ever have in his life.

Lenore was, putting it mildly, a *revelation*: an attentive, active lover who looked to John's pleasure in each movement, each touch, but who also joyfully indulged herself in every gratification John was able to offer. He felt a little hopeless in the burning heat of her love, but he gladly did his best to keep up. She seemed to know *all* of the things John liked, and how he liked them, and he never had to tell her any of those things. And again, without asking for his input, she also performed acts with him that he had always *wanted* to do with a woman but had never been close enough with anybody to try. John had been with some women in his lifetime, but he knew of nothing that could compare with what he experienced that night in Lenore's loving arms.

It was a long time before they slept, but when they did, it was when they were completely exhausted, entwined together in the same bed. Lenore twitched in her sleep, her terrible dreams returning, as John held her close and stroked her hair. His own dreams were also unpleasant, all war and death, but they made it through the night with no evil visits or interruptions, still wrapped in each other's arms when morning came.

AFTER THEY DRESSED and ate another morning meal of undiscernible food—this time, some radishes and white beans—John asked Lenore if she would again join him in town. She responded by saying that she *would* accompany him to town, if that was what he wished to do today, but she proposed an alternative plan: "We can always go back to town another day, John. Why don't we stay here at the manor, perhaps looking after one another, all day long, right here in this cozy camp?" She pointed to the beds, and winked slyly, saying, "I promise you that I didn't use *all* of my tricks last night. I do know of a few more things that we will enjoy trying."

John laughed, thinking that there couldn't possibly be anything left in the world that they could try together that they did not do the previous night. "That sounds exhausting...and, no doubt, quite wonderful, my lady...but you must know that I won't leave the commission unfinished."

"Yes, I do know that, but I had to try. We don't need to actively seek the things that will bring us pain, you know. Cartwright won't return for a long time, and you could easily slow your investigation a bit, without any impact. A few more days, just us—and I repeat, mostly in this bed!—but occasionally pushing back together against whatever might be thrown at us from the manor proper?"

John thought of the jelly jars of kerosene in the basement. He wasn't going down there to check, but he was fairly sure that two remained, and those two were the ones with the fiery scenes with skulls and dark figures: a man and a woman, one in each corner of the basement. He felt that he was *meant* to investigate both of the fires in River's Edge, discovering the meanings of each and somehow completing an arcane sequence that would do...what? Maybe it was his path to *escaping* Everbridge Manor, a way to get him and Lenore away from the continual hauntings—these repeated, physical and emotional attacks— on these cursed grounds. "Sorry, Lenore, but I must see to it. There's a reason we're being funneled to these terrible crimes, and I mean to find out what it is."

At that moment, John's horse came walking out of the front of the manor, lifting up its hooves to clear the smashed door. "Oh, perfect," John said. "We can take His Majesty."

"I'd rather leave him here, if you don't mind. I don't want you to—" She sighed, and stopped her sentence. John walked over, took the horse's reins, and walked it back to the camp. "Shall we go?" he asked.

Lenore nodded, and they walked with the horse over the bridge to head to town.

_________ ෙ ◎ ෙ _________

Lenore was uncharacteristically sad as they walked toward River's Edge. She clutched his arm tightly, and generally stayed quite close to John as they traversed the road. They passed the inert cottages and eventually made it to the main street of River's Edge.

Little had changed since the previous day. The businesses and buildings were all dark and empty, and it took only a minute for them to reach the burned-out office they had investigated the previous day. The same pillar of smoke that had constantly persisted at this spot was still here. Everything about the office indicated that the fire that destroyed it had only ended a few hours earlier; the wood glowed orange all over, and the heat from what remained of the structure was profound. John could smell burned flesh, and held his wrist up to his nose. Lenore stayed in the street with the horse, as John walked up to the threshold to take another look at the scene. He didn't need her encouragement this time; he just walked to the office door and peered in. He drew in an audible breath and said, simply, "No."

The fat man's smoldering body was back at the burned mahogany desk, atop his ruined chair. The woman's body, with the letter opener protruding from her eye, was again sprawled on the soot-covered floor. John repeated, "No," as he stepped inside to look through the hole in the wall into the warehouse... where the warehouse worker's torn body was again on the floor. He and Lenore had buried all three of these people yesterday, and yet their bodies had returned. It was exactly the same, approaching the building today, as it had been yesterday.

John walked back over to where Lenore was standing. He was visibly shaken, and she was, too. She had tears on her face. When he said, "What does this mean?" Lenore just folded her arm into his and pulled him close, saying nothing. Further down the street, at the inn across from the schoolhouse, another pillar of smoke rose, and John watched it for a minute, saying nothing but wearing a serious expression.

John let go of Lenore and began walking down the street toward the other smoking building. He picked up his pace with each step, and Lenore hurried behind, towing His Majesty, trying to catch up. The schoolhouse was soon on their right, and a small park on the left. The last building on the street, next to the park, was the town inn. A column of black smoke rose slowly from its location. When John reached it, he didn't pause in any way before stepping directly into the smoldering ruin. Lenore stayed outside.

The inn had just suffered complete devastation from a fire that ended only a few hours earlier. The roof was mostly gone, and the rooms were barely delineated from one another because large portions of the wooden walls had burned away. The heavy, wooden front desk was just a pile of ashes and splintered wood. John knew right where to go to find what there was to see; he had been here before.

He entered the first guest room, where he found three burned corpses. A tall man with the remains of some sort of black hat burned to his head had died with his body pointing toward the door. A woman was nearby, with an axe embedded in her chest. John had a hard time looking at the third corpse: a man with one outstretched arm reaching toward the doorway. This man's head was skewed, as if it had been squashed, either before or after he died. Looking at this man caused John's stomach to twist; he nearly vomited the small breakfast that he had eaten earlier. All three corpses were burned and unidentifiable.

John did not linger in this room, heading quickly to the one next door to it. In this room, a small woman and a small child had burned up in a bed. They had apparently been sleeping together when the fire consumed the whole building, and for some reason they did not move out to safety.

John walked back to the street, where Lenore was crying, standing next to His Majesty.

"The commission," John said. "It's just a trick, isn't it?"

Lenore said nothing, just looked over at him sadly as another tear trailed down from her eye.

"You tried to tell me," John said, "but I didn't listen."

"Yes, you're right," Lenore said quietly. "Cartwright's commission is nonsense. They give it to you just to make you—"

A few spindly trees in the park had survived the blaze next door, but right at that moment they burst into flames. It was as if someone had ignited some gas burners, with three brittle, leafless trees right in the middle of them. John exclaimed, "What in heaven's name is that?"

Lenore stopped talking. John said, "Those trees, sparking into flame...it's another warning, isn't it?"

Lenore nodded slowly, her bottom lip quivering. John said, "The commission exists only to make me come here, to make me look upon this, right?"

"I'm sorry, John," Lenore managed to say, in a quiet voice. "I wish I could tell you more. I wish I could *help* you more." The flames that had ignited the three trees in the park began to die down.

He looked down the street to where the road ran out of town, past Everbridge Manor, to Junction City beyond. "I must leave," he said firmly.

Lenore shook her head, her chest hitching with her cries. She stepped over to him and grabbed both of his arms, pulling him close. "Please don't go, John. We still have some more time, there's no need to go! You can just keep your conclusions to yourself for another day, maybe even two!"

"No, Lenore. I'm starting to understand. I have to leave this place. It seems to exist only to bring me pain, to taunt me with the memories of things I cannot recall and, quite possibly, terrible things I have done. This place is *wrong*. It feels like a *story*, not a life. So I must see if Junction City is any different."

Lenore put her arms around him, burying her face in his chest as her sobs grew more intense. She was becoming frantic, weeping and talking quickly. "Stay, John, please! I can't talk to you about any of *this*, but there are many other things we *can* say! We can eat those silly coconuts, and have some laughs! We can spend another night in each other's arms! I know you would enjoy that! We don't need to talk at all...or...or we can talk about *earlier* times, times that have nothing to do with these bodies...these crimes...nothing to do with Everbridge Manor. You can tell me the story of when the captain fell off his horse into the Main River that one time and lost one of his boots!"

John shook his head. "You know I would truly enjoy *all* of those things, Lenore, but that just strengthens my resolve. I haven't told you that story about the captain...how could you know it?"

"I'm not...I'm not allowed to say. I'm so sorry, John, for all of it. But please...please tell me you'll stay! I love you! If you believe nothing else I say, please at least believe *that*. Won't you come back to the manor, and find out if you can love me back?"

John mounted His Majesty as Lenore clutched desperately at the reins. "I already do, Lenore. But I must ride." He kicked the horse and pulled away from her.

She called after him, "You won't make it, John! There's nothing out there!"

He rode through town toward the river, turned left, and headed in the direction of Junction City.

JOHN DROVE His Majesty at a fast gallop, leaning forward as the brittle forest whipped by on one side, the black river on the other. Occasionally, the river would fall out of sight behind some trees, but by following the road further along, it would reappear again. As he progressed, the sky grew darker, not with impending rain, but with...just darkness. John was becoming winded, the further away from Everbridge Manor he got, but he attributed it to the rigors of horse-riding, and pressed on, faster and faster. They were galloping away from River's Edge for a half hour, then an hour, as trees and road and gloom rushed past in a blur.

John had travelled this road, back and forth from River's Edge to Junction City, many times in his life, but his first time had been when he travelled it with his mother, back when he was five years old. They had left their small room behind the cobbler's shop, carrying most everything they owned in a sack, heading to River's Edge to find "that rat," his father. As John drove his horse ever onward, both of them panting, John *remembered*. He remembered *all of it*. These memories came to him with the same force of his dreams of late: fully experienced, inescapable. He remembered what happened after his mother knocked on the door of Everbridge Manor that fateful evening, remembered what happened in the manor right after that, and what happened later that night in the office in River's Edge. It came to him with the force of a physical punch in the gut, and he exclaimed in pain when it hit him. "No...oh no," he cried. "No, Lenore."

It was becoming harder and harder to breathe, and also harder to focus his eyes on his surroundings. He felt he could no longer blame it on the exertion of riding a horse at a hard gallop for an extended period. He could hear His Majesty, also struggling to breathe, the horse's pace slowing.

John smacked the reins on His Majesty's flank, shouting, "Hyah!", driving the animal onward. He gritted his teeth, suddenly feeling tears on his own cheeks. His memories—so many new ones, so many terrible ones—were crushing him.

Another time when John journeyed on this road was when he returned, recently, to confront Kitty after hearing that she was going to sell Everbridge Manor. Previously, his recollections of this encounter ended just after he decided to undertake the trip, but now he recalled what happened after that. It was all so clear, even the end of it, the horrible end. He remembered riding His Majesty in the *other* direction down this long road, toward River's Edge. He remembered approaching the Inn there, late at night, and meeting Kitty when he called at the front lobby. When he remembered what happened in Kitty and Rooster's room, his head snapped back as if he had been punched. He cried out into the darkness, "No! Please...no, it must not be!" and felt his whole body hitching and spasming with wracking sobs.

As His Majesty progressed forward, slower and slower despite John's provocations, John experienced the most-intense emotional pain he had ever known. This feeling of devastation was accompanied by a distinct inability to breathe, and a near-complete dimming of his surroundings. The road ahead, supposedly leading to Junction City, as well as the road behind, leading back to Everbridge Manor, were both becoming lost in blackness.

His Majesty stopped, and John thought that the animal would fall over. This was the end for them, out here in the shadow, the nothing. He and the horse both drew long, loud, ragged breaths, each one providing the breather with less and less oxygen. His Majesty swayed beneath him.

John thought to turn around, to head back to the manor before his fate became sealed. But he was sure that he had gone too far...like learning, after you have dived deep in some water, that you swam down too far to have enough breath left to last you back to the surface.

John was now convinced that all of this was *not real*, and that he was not insane for thinking so. Being at the edge of all existence makes that conclusion—*not real*, so *not real*—quite obvious. The road before him, which was no longer visible, did *not* lead to Junction City. Junction City no longer existed. This road was a road to *nowhere*, a place where the world—whatever this world was—ended.

Actually, he shouldn't kid himself, here at the very end; he knew exactly what this world was.

The darkness closed in all around, absolute; life was an afterimage on his eyeballs in the night, a candle that was just blown out, now with only blackness all around.

He pulled the reins to turn His Majesty in the other direction. The giant animal was reluctant to move, as it was currently suffocating. John would not be conscious for much longer. He jabbed the horse's flanks with his heels, and it turned. It also started to move, slowly, forward, along the surface of the blank, dark nothingness in front of them.

John wrapped the reins tightly around the saddle horn and then around his wrists, and let the blackness take him.

AFTER KITTY CAME to Lenore's bedroom to tell her of their visitor, Lenore walked to the top of the stairs above the foyer and looked down. Below, in the entryway, the matron was arguing with an irate older woman, who had one hand raised in an aggressive "see, here!" pointing gesture, and the other one holding a large round sack over her shoulder. The woman was probably forty years old, with long, messily-braided hair, streaked with grey. She wore a charcoal-colored dress with a ruffled skirt that was threadbare in some places, cheaply repaired in others. A little boy, about Kitty's age, perhaps just a little older, peeked out from behind her.

"I demand to see *Bertram*!" the woman was shouting, and the matron was trying to tell her over and over that The Master was not presently at home. The matron's face was beet-red at the exertion, and Lenore thought she could hear the servant's ragged breathing, from mid-way down the stairs.

The woman would not take "no" for an answer, instead shouting, "But I am his *wife*!"

Lenore was exhausted from confrontations in her life, but came down the stairway and engaged anyway. "Madam, may I ask who you are?"

The visitor rustled around in the front pocket of her skirt and pulled out a folded piece of paper, which she proceeded to wave to the rooftops. "Bertram is my husband! I have this certificate of marriage to prove it! That dirty rat left me and our son to rot in poverty back in Junction City!"

Lenore might have been inclined to disbelieve this ragged woman and her sudden, shocking statements, but she had no trouble whatsoever believing these claims. The Master was a terrible human being, whom Lenore knew failed to take even the basic steps needed to be *considered* a human being. Lenore thought to herself, "Well, you can certainly have him, I'll not fight you for him," but instead said, "How long ago was this?"

The woman shouted, "Five, almost six, years ago, when I became pregnant with my John, here!" The boy behind her looked up sheepishly at Lenore, Kitty, and the matron, but said nothing.

Again, this all sounded right in character for Lenore's dear husband, though it occurred to her that, if this angry woman was correct, The Master was *no longer her husband*. You can't marry a second woman while still betrothed to a previous one. Lenore felt a flicker of hope ignite in her heart. She might just find a way to get herself and Kitty away from the beast who constantly attacked them.

She raised her hands to calm the woman, and then moved

to take the woman's arm and lead her, kindly, to the parlor. "Please calm down, madam. Let's go to the parlor and talk. We can have some tea. May I ask your name?"

The woman, however, was unwilling to stand down from her rage, shouting, "We will do no such thing! Now...where... is...Bertram?"

The matron, perhaps emboldened by the same weak glimmer of hope that Lenore experienced, spoke up: "He has an office in River's Edge. It's on the main street, just across from the general store." And then, as if to help this ragged woman avoid her initial serving of rage when she first addressed him, she added, "He likes to be called 'The Master,' now, though."

"I'll show *him* who the master is," the angry woman shouted, "when I find him!"

Lenore thought this was overly-bold talk, but did not know the shabby woman enough to determine if it could be right. The woman certainly seemed agitated enough to confront The Master that way, but it would probably not work out well. She said, "All right, madam, I can take you to Bertram in town. Please give me a moment to go upstairs and change."

"What's wrong with the clothes you're wearing?" The woman's clothes were rumpled and old, in far worse shape than the pristine green dress that Lenore was currently wearing, but Lenore thought to herself, "You bring up a good point, madam." Instead of saying that out loud, she said, "These clothes are not *town* clothes. I must change, but I will be swift about it. Please sit by the fire in the parlor, and I will be down oh-so-quickly." And with that, Lenore ascended the stairs without looking back. Over her shoulder, she heard the woman moving, under protest and muttering the whole time, into the parlor.

Wearing house clothes to town would enrage The Master, Lenore knew, but a mighty confrontation was brewing regardless of her choice of outfit. She quickly changed into a town-appropriate, charcoal-colored skirt, paired with a stiff grey blouse with a lace collar. The night would be chilly, so she added a beige sweater with embroidered flowers to the ensemble, and hurriedly descended the stairs.

The woman was sitting—awkwardly, as if she could not find a comfortable angle—in one of the parlor chairs near the fire, with her son and her sack sitting on the ground nearby, next to Kitty. These children looked a little like each other, Lenore thought, which made sense since they purportedly shared the same father. When the woman saw Lenore approaching, with her town outfit *just so*, she spit, "Well, aren't you a pretty picture, missy!" and beckoned to her son. "Come along, John." She stood up, pointedly leaving her giant sack where it was, grabbed her son's hand, and marched to the entryway and then out the front door.

Lenore leaned down, gave Kitty a kiss on the forehead, and said, "Stay with Clara, Kitty. Mind her, please, my love. I should be back soon." Lenore looked over at the matron, who was still red-faced and looking slightly ill. Lenore, who always tried to call the servant by her first name, said, "Clara, wish me luck."

Outside, Lenore met up with the ragged woman who claimed to be The Master's first—and current—wife, and with the woman's son in tow, the three of them walked to town. It was a short walk, perhaps ten minutes, and the whole time the woman muttered and barked and mostly refused to provide any useful answers to questions. She still refused to give her name, even when Lenore politely offered her own. As they neared River's Edge, she gave Lenore a disturbing warning to stay out of her way, growling that she would get her Bertram back, regardless of what Lenore thought or did. The woman became more and more agitated as they walked; Lenore thought that she seemed a little unhinged.

They made it to River's Edge in short order, and when they got to The Master's business office, the woman burst right in. Their obese husband was ensconced at his giant desk in the center of the room, opening mail with an elaborate golden letter opener. A heavy, somewhat illegible ledger was open before him, illuminated via a lit kerosene lamp on the edge of the desk. He wore a gleaming, enormous, brown waistcoat, a long-sleeved white shirt, and the type of colored ascot of which he was fond, but which made him look like a dimwit. Tonight's ascot was yellow. The woman pulled her son into the room with her, and Lenore followed behind them.

"What is—" The Master sputtered. He demanded, "What is the meaning of this?"

The ragged woman stepped up to the desk, her folded evidence of legal marriage held up in one hand, and placed the other hand on edge of the desk, shouting right in the man's red face: "It's me, Bertram! It's me, your Winifred! I've come here with your boy, after you ran—"

The Master reached up, grabbed her by her gray-streaked braid, and yanked her down, slamming her head on the desk before she could finish her sentence. A semi-circle of blood sprayed out from her mouth onto the open, top page of the ledger. The woman slumped forward toward the desktop, and then slid all the way to the floor in a heap, her eyes half-closed, blood running down her chin from her mouth and nose. Lenore pushed little John back out the front door, saying, "Stay out there, my love," and closing it before stepping back into the office to look after the woman whose name she finally knew was Winifred.

Lenore bent down to see to Winifred, noting right away that the woman was still breathing. Her eyes fluttered open and closed. The Master growled, "Begone! I have problems enough, not having to deal with this nonsense, Lenore." He took a handkerchief from the pocket of his massive waistcoat and wiped at the ledger.

Lenore looked up at him and said, "You might have killed her."

"What of it, and why should I care one way or the other?" he shouted. "I'll do what I want, and none of the likes of *you* can tell me what to do." He looked back down to his papers, as if there was nothing at all happening out of the ordinary. "Someone has sent double kerosene and double peaches, the fools, and now I have to distribute the whole lot!"

Lenore came around the side of the desk and spoke down to him. She did not notice the front door of the office opening up again. "This woman claims that you were already married to her!"

The Master was bubbling with rage now. He would not endure Lenore standing above him so—fists on hips, demanding, judging—for very long. "I was, the stupid cow! And then she went and got herself with child. All of these foul, shrieking children, who wants them?"

Right when Lenore said, "But what of—", The Master grabbed her by the front of her clothes with his left hand, and rocketed his giant right hand straight into her face. She stumbled back, dazed, into the wall between the office and the warehouse next door, knocking a kerosene lamp from a shelf. The unlit lamp shattered, spilling oil all over the plywood wall, floor, and desk area. And then, while Lenore was still recovering, The Master heaved himself up from his chair and was upon her, strangling her while pummeling her face and neck over and over, easily using his massive bulk to overpower her. Now this, *this* was something Lenore understood: it was the same type of beating she had previously endured from him, but this time, she feared that he would kill her.

Winifred peered up over the top of the desk, apparently recovering a small share of her wits. And the next thing Lenore knew, Winifred was right there, too, having somehow decided to wobble over and join the fight. Only Winifred wasn't fighting The Master, she was fighting Lenore. "You leave him be, missy!" she shouted. "He's mine!" She was not effective in her attacks, having had her face smashed on a desk a few minutes earlier, but two against one made for bad odds. It was a bloody, three-person jumble for ten seconds, and Lenore was easily going to lose the fight. She took one last, desperate swing, managing to smash the base of her hand up into The Master's bulbous nose.

The Master fell backward, still holding Lenore by the hair as he went, landing hard in his office chair and pulling her near to him. The lower half of his face was covered in his blood, but now he was laughing. He pulled her right up to his face and slurred, "I *own* you, Lenore. You have *no power* here. I could kill you...both of you...and nobody...nobody...would take a bit of notice."

In the close quarters behind the desk, holding her hair tightly in his left hand, The Master gleefully hit Lenore in the left eye. His fat hand was so huge, it was like being smashed by a log. Her hands ineffectively pounded against him, scrabbled around the chair and the desk, as she lost her strength. Winifred was behind her, too, pummeling Lenore in the back. The Master hit Lenore again.

Lenore's hand found the letter opener that he had been using when they entered the office, and, in between his blows, she plunged it deep into the side of his neck. The Master sputtered and cried out. A fierce jet of blood sprayed out from his neck, the kind of foul emission that occurs when a red bug is stomped, followed by a second spray, this one less grand. He brought his right hand up to the blade, but that was the last thing he did, because he lost his life before he could pull it out. His huge head slumped forward onto the desk. Lenore stumbled backwards, coughing and holding one hand to her face where she had been repeatedly hit.

Winifred took the lantern that The Master had on his desk and threw it at Lenore. Lenore was groggy herself, but she was just able to dodge it, and the glass and metal device smashed on the wall behind her instead, spreading its fuel and flames in all directions. When the flames came in contact with all of the oil that had been spilled from the first lamp, everything behind the desk and associated with the plywood wall blazed up immediately.

Winifred pulled the letter opener from The Master's dead neck and came at Lenore. They scuffled behind the desk, where flames were rising all around them. This shabby woman's dream of reuniting with her wayward husband was never going to come true, and she was furious. "What have you done, missy? What have you done?" Winifred swung the bloody letter opener around with wild eyes, shouting, "I'll still have what is his, when *you* are gone!" Lenore defended herself, grabbing the woman's arms, wondering if hitting her head on the desk had knocked something loose in Winifred.

The fire raged through the whole office; they needed to get out. Yet Winifred kept attacking Lenore, grappling over the letter opener and eventually pulling her arm free to swing the weapon in all directions. After avoiding several swipes that nearly stabbed into her, Lenore ducked away, using her elbow to knock the ragged woman's arm up and away from her; the momentum of the blade continued, but in a direction Winifred did not intend, and Winifred ended up stabbing herself directly in the eye. She fell down in a heap, her clothes starting to burn immediately. Winifred stared up at Lenore from the other eye, but there was no spark of life there.

John, suddenly an orphan at five years old, was standing in the open doorway, having seen the entire fight. Lenore dodged the rising flames and headed to the door, scooping John up and running out of the building. Behind them, a double order of kerosene, shipped in jelly jars, and stacked in the warehouse on the wall adjacent to The Master's desk, ignited from the burning plywood it shared with the office.

Next door, the warehouse manager, an easy-going man named Julian, slept in the utility cot that he kept in the warehouse. He had recently and thoroughly enjoyed a single tin of sliced peaches before snuggling down. A sound sleeper, he heard none of the fighting in the office next door prior to the explosion. He was killed in his sleep when the kerosene jars detonated.

The explosion blew Lenore and John forward, where they landed in the middle of the street. Lenore got right up, grabbed little John—not by the hand but by the body—and ran, now crying, with him to Everbridge Manor.

She knew there would be no escape with Kitty, and this devastated her. The townspeople would string Lenore up for killing The Master and Winifred. No explanation would be sufficient to save her. She believed Kitty would come out of it as well as could be expected; her daughter would own the manor, based on The Master's taunting declarations of the condition of his will, and she would probably be well taken care of by Clara, the matron.

They reached the manor and entered the front door, where they were met in the entryway by a distraught Clara and a confused Kitty. "Madam," the matron said, her face growing red from all of the stressful events around her. "What in heaven's name has happened?"

Lenore nudged John forward, saying, "Clara, this is John. He is Bertram's son. Please take care of him. And my Kitty."

The red-faced matron was confused, clutching a hand to her chest. "How?" she asked. "What do you mean? How can you ask this of me?"

Lenore didn't answer. She touched Kitty's face with her hand and walked up the wide stairway for the final time, crying and not looking back. Behind her, the matron seemed to understand a part of what was being asked, and called out, "Madam, wait!" The servant now had an idea of what Lenore was about to do, and said, quietly, "This...this is just evil."

At the top of the stairs, Lenore paused for a moment to look at the ridiculous portrait of the foul man who had just died while trying to beat her to death. She pulled the large portrait down from its hook as she passed, ripping one of the corners of the canvas.

From the second floor, a small stairway lead to the high roof of Everbridge Manor. Lenore exited the rooftop door onto the shingled roof, walked straight to the edge, and pitched herself off.

Below, Kitty, John, and the matron were still standing in the entryway as Lenore's body smashed into the rosemary bushes and the ground in the front of the house, making a terrifying crunch as she died. Kitty exclaimed, "Oh, Momma!", ran over to her mother's body, and began to cry.

The matron screamed, high-pitched and directly in John's ear, but then transitioned to a strangled, gasping croak. She coughed once, and clutched both hands to her uniform, and looked down at John in an expression of contorted pain. Her face was already beet red, and then her eyes turned red, too. And then she died from the heart attack that Lenore always feared for her, her limp, dead body falling backwards toward the front stairway.

JOHN LEFT Junction City in the late evening, having heard from Rolf that he could find Kitty at the River's Edge Inn. He rode down the main road along the river, arriving at the small riverside town in just a few hours by driving at a hard clip. It was just before midnight when he rode up the main street, past the municipal building, general store, offices, and warehouse, to the town Inn, which was across the street from the schoolhouse.

The night sky was clear, and there was a mostly-full moon, which illuminated John's surroundings. There was a small park on one side of the inn, probably used by the schoolchildren on some days, and a stump for chopping wood on the other side. A stack of split wood stood beside the stump, and a hefty axe protruded from it.

The Inn only had two rooms in it, along with the room where the Innkeeper herself stayed. John entered the Inn, finding the entry lobby empty. There was a cowbell hanging on the wall near the front desk, and he struck it, once, with the tiny hammer that was attached. He wasn't concerned that it was the middle of the night. He was in a hurry to talk to his sister, and he needed to find out which room she was staying in.

The door of the nearest guest room opened, and his step-sister Kitty peeked out. John had not seen her in several years, and those years had not been kind. He was surprised to see that Kitty was thin and pale; she did not look well. She called over, "John. John."

"Oh, hello, Kitty," he said.

"Try to stay quiet, they're sleeping. The Innkeeper told me to keep a watch out for customers."

"Is that your room?" John asked.

"Yes, this way," she replied, beckoning him to the open door. "In here, John."

John entered the room, finding it already occupied by a tall man with aggressive sideburns and a mostly-bald head. The man pulled on a bowler hat and approached John quickly, getting into John's space in short order. "Well, you must be the famous militia-man brother that Kitty's always dronin' on about!" His voice was far too loud for someone standing five feet away, and Kitty shushed him. "Keep it down, Rooster! You know they're sleeping!"

Kitty sat down at a chair on the side of the room, near a desk with a kerosene lantern on it, and her body language suggested that she was getting situated for a difficult conversa-tion. She motioned toward the tall bowler-hat man, and said,

"John, this is Rooster. He's my...*husband*." John was taken aback; Kitty did not seem like the marrying kind. And the pause she took before the word "husband" stood out to John, making him wonder if Kitty was somehow regretting whatever choices she had made to end up married to this person.

Rooster leaned toward John and stuck out a skinny hand. The next thing he shouted clarified the condition of their marriage right away: "She means 'common law husband,' Johnny. 'Common law,' like *unofficial*, right? Put 'er there, brother!"

John briefly shook Rooster's hand, hoping that the gesture would allow the tall man to move out of his personal space. To hurry that possibility along, John stepped over to the other room chair, at which point, Rooster sat on the bed, leaning back on his elbows.

Kitty said, "John, it's good to see you," but the strange way she phrased it made John wonder if he wasn't going to like the rest of what she had to say. She could not sit still on the chair, fidgeting and anxiously scratching at herself. John wondered what was going on with her health. She said, "I want to talk to you about Everbridge Manor."

John nodded. "Yes, I heard a rumor that you want to sell it. That is why I came as soon as I heard."

On the bed, Rooster affected a sarcastic look, and said, "What was the hurry, Johnny-boy? It's not like you have any say in what Kitty does with *her* property."

"I would hope she would listen to my advice, as her brother, who grew up with her in that home."

"But who doesn't *own* that home," Rooster clarified with a smirk, none too helpfully.

John wasn't to be baited so easily, instead addressing Kitty by saying, "It's true that I don't own the manor. But may I ask why you think you need to sell it?"

Kitty sighed. "I need the money. Rooster wants to—" she

stopped. "We. *We* want to follow our dream...to open up a tavern with the proceeds of the sale."

"A tavern? I thought you wanted to buy a horse ranch, or what was it? Open a school for troubled teenagers."

Rooster sat forward and laughed at this, a mean, hearty, "Ha!" Kitty looked none too pleased with this reaction, and Rooster just settled back, saying, "Oh, I thought that was a joke."

John continued. "Well, no, it wasn't a joke. Kitty had plenty of dreams of what to do with the money if she sold the manor, and it never included opening a tavern. Where would this supposed tavern be?"

"It's right here in River's Edge, down near the docks," Kitty replied. "We've already agreed to the sale, and we'll get the money day after tomorrow. Rooster is going to—"

John interrupted, "What? You've already agreed to the sale? Is there a way to stop it? Take it back? I truly don't want you selling our childhood home to buy some sort of...tavern!"

Rooster stood up, a scowl on his face. He was demonstrably taller than John, who had to angle his head quite a ways up to see the other man's angry face. "What do you mean, saying, 'some sort of tavern' like that? I don't think I like your tone!"

John stood. Kitty rose as well, moving in front of Rooster, one hand on each man, saying, in as quiet a voice as she could manage, "Now, boys, let's not let this get all heated. We need to agree about the *house*."

Now that things had gotten "all heated," Rooster seemed much more comfortable in his standing. "You don't need to get all high-and-mighty like that, Johnny," he said, leaning forward. "I might just have to *pop* you one, settle you right down."

"Well, sir," John said, squaring his feet to the man standing right in front of him, trying to stay prepared for anything, "I don't think a 'common law husband' should be strong-arming my sister into liquidating her only property for purposes of—"

Rooster jacked his right fist out at John's face, which John dodged easily. The tall man swung again, from the side, and again, John ducked it. Kitty said, "John! Stop it! And please stay quiet!" But Rooster was becoming enraged by missing his attacks, and he was not going to stop.

Next, John punched the tall man straight in the nose, one solid shot, a right hand jab. The tall man went down on one knee, holding his hand over his nose. Kitty shouted, "John! Enough!" as Rooster growled, "I think I'll have to hurt you for that, Johnny."

The tall man sprung up to his feet, bowling John backwards into a long dresser, which jammed forcefully into his spine. While John was reeling from this impact with the dresser, Rooster hit John on both sides of his head at once, staggering him with a ringing blow, all the while scowling with fierce, rising hatred. When John managed to get up to counter-attack, Kitty was there, holding down John's hands to keep him from connecting with Rooster. But still, even with Kitty intervening against him, John's training as a militia-man and a constable enabled him to throw her off and connect with the tall man's face, staggering Rooster several times. Blood ran from Rooster's mouth and nose. They fought like this for almost a minute, with Rooster's ability to fight flagging in reverse proportion to his anger. He was not winning the fight, yet he was becoming more and more enraged as the encounter went on. Kitty disappeared from the room as John continued to rain blows down on her aggressive "common law" husband.

When Kitty returned, she had the axe from the stump outside the inn. John thought that maybe she meant to threaten them, to get them to stand down from their fighting, but Rooster grabbed it from her. He had apparently formed his own ideas about how to end the fight once and for all, and the appearance of a deadly weapon fit right in. John grabbed the upper part of the axe handle, right near the blade, as it swung down toward him, and he and Rooster wrestled the sharp instrument inches away from their two faces as they fought over control of the handle. Kitty was there, too, interfering everywhere in the fight, from all directions, but Rooster elbowed her away, feeling like he was now gaining the upper hand.

As they were wrestling back and forth, John suddenly wrenched the head of the axe in an unexpected direction, and Rooster loosened his hold at just that moment to prepare a different angle of attack. John gained the entire axe, yanking it to the right, its blade flashing in front of him for just a fraction of a second before the sharp part it ended up embedded in Kitty's sternum.

Kitty's eyes widened, and she looked down at the axe sticking out of her. She whispered, "What have you done, John?" And then his sister fell backward, gasping, and landing on the ground, where she quickly became quite still. Kitty's blood seeped onto the wooden floor in an ever-widening circle around her now-dead body. As John stood there, standing over her, shocked and reeling from what he had just done, Rooster smashed him over the head with one of the small chairs. John went down, next to Kitty, and Rooster stomped his booted foot right down on John's ear, full force, in a killing blow. John's head cracked in two, across the top and back, and everything became murky as he quickly hurtled toward death.

Far, far away from John, Rooster growled, "Now look what you've gone and done, Johnny. This is a real mess."

As the small circle of light in front of John's eyes shrunk, Rooster appeared to be flying around the room in a rage, trying to figure out what to do. He was talking to himself as he tried to find a way past the murder that just happened. "They'll have *me* for this, you fool! You've done it now, Johnny-boy! I'll never get away from it, not after that business back in Four Corners."

John felt some liquid on his face, and was no longer present enough to know that Rooster had started to fling the kerosene from the desk lamp all around the room, on top of John, on top of Kitty. John was unable to move his body, except for a small twitch that he could make with his hand. Rooster muttered to himself, "What am I supposed to do about the brat? It's not like *I* can take care of him."

Rooster then struck a match, saying to himself "Kitty just *had* to have a baby. Doesn't even talk, the creepy little monster. Serves me right for agreeing." He threw the lit match on top of Kitty and John, and everything around them started to go up in flames. John could not feel any of it. "I'll wake up the innkeeper, get him from her. Hmm, wait...maybe I can convince *her* to look after him."

Rooster moved to leave, and, as his last act before dying, John angled his finger upward and touched the man's pant-leg as he went by. Rooster looked down, saw the unexpected move-ment, said, "Get off!", and kicked away with that leg.

The floor in that area of the burning room was unexpect-edly slippery with Kitty's blood, and Rooster's other foot slipped out from under him. When he fell, he cracked his temple on the nearby small chair, falling unconscious rather than executing his hasty plan of rousing his son from the arms of the sleeping innkeeper and fleeing.

The innkeeper was a woman of over ninety years old named Dorothea. She lived in the room next to the one where Rooster had just fallen. She slept like the dead, always wrapped in a heavy shawl to ward off the chill. She had her arms and shawl tightly encircled around Theo, Kitty's child of five years old, as the inn burned down around them all.

John became conscious again as his horse walked across the bridge into the courtyard of Everbridge Manor. He opened his eyes, seeing a bumpy view of the trees on the other side of the river. His body was being pulled along the ground, his wrists having been lashed to the saddle horn back at the edge of the world. He must have fallen off His Majesty when he passed out from lack of oxygen back there, but the horse survived and travelled the rest of the way, dragging John along the dusty road back to familiar ground.

Across the river, right where John was looking, every one of the trees suddenly burst into flames. It was the same surprising ignition that had happened in the park in River's Edge earlier, except now it was every tree in sight. John pulled up on the straps binding his wrists, gaining his feet and unwrapping himself. The impossible flaming trees made a ring of fire all around the manor, and the trees started to move closer.

Lenore came to him in the courtyard and wrapped her arms around him in a huge hug. He was stiff and sore from being dragged along the road from Junction City. "John!" Lenore exclaimed. "I'm so glad you made it back! This part is so much easier if it is the both of us."

Everbridge Manor had seen better days since the last time John had been there. Every window was smashed, even the upstairs ones, from the force of some detonations inside the house. John knew which detonations those were. He thought of the jelly jar with the dark woman carrying the thin blade, and the one with the dark man carrying an axe...surmising that, since he had discovered who the murderers were in River's Edge, those two remaining jars of kerosene had exploded. The courtyard was littered with broken glass and wood framing from those blasts. The whole house was sagging in on itself slightly, its timbers lubricated with the contents of four giant jars of kerosene. And now, a ring of fire formed by flaming trees was marching closer.

Lenore said, "After the last two vessels broke, the trees stayed where they were...so I knew you were still alive. Clever, tying your hands to your horse like that. Come, let's go inside. We don't have much more time."

"Time before what?"

"Before the *end*!" Lenore said. "You must have figured out what's going on by now, what this phony version of Everbridge Manor is! John, do you know what we are...*where* we are?"

John nodded, saying, "Yes, I do. It's obvious. You and I are both dead, and this is Hell."

Lenore nodded back. "That's exactly right. A special Hell, created just for us, from all of the pieces of our crimes. What else?"

John sighed and continued. "And now we're at the end of some kind of insane punishment sequence, where we pay a painful, ultimate price."

The circle of flaming trees was slowly constricting, like a knot in a rope being pulled tighter and tighter. The ring had made it to the middle of the bridge. John thought to himself, "Look! Retaliatory trees!" and managed a small smile.

John looked up at the roofline of the house, where each one of their victims stood, standing still and scowling down at them. Despite some of these people being decent human beings in life, innocent victims in some cases, they were now all glaring fiercely at John and Lenore. John saw his father, the fat man who demanded to be called The Master, wearing his ascot, and brandishing a heavy piece of wood that looked like it had been broken off of the main stair railing. He saw his mother, wearing her threadbare clothes and holding the letter opener with blackened blood on the handle. Next to John's mother stood the warehouse man, holding two sealed cans of peaches, and next, the matron, who gripped a giant kitchen knife. The four of them had been killed, one way or another, by Lenore. Her crimes had occurred twenty-five years earlier, when John had been five years old.

Rooster, he of the bowler hat and abundant sideburns,

stood menacingly up there on the roof, smacking one fist into the other. Nearby, John's half-sister Kitty glared angrily at him, holding her axe in two hands. Kitty's son was beside her, again pressing his hands to the sides of his head and sticking out his tongue. Lastly, the ancient lady innkeeper stared down with black eyes full of hate. These last four had been killed, through some combination of bad luck or bad choices, by John.

Lenore said, "Normally, the ones you killed will mostly bother you, and the ones I killed bother me, but now, all bets are off. They will *all* come for us."

"But...to what end?" John asked. "We're already dead!"

"Right now, they want us to *burn*."

The burning trees were nearly upon them. The ring of flames was impenetrable. Lenore said, "You have to trust me here, John. We need to get inside, and head to the roof."

All eight of the people on the roof turned back toward the house at once, and ran to the rooftop stair. If they meant to attack, they would all be upon them in short order.

John wondered if there was some method of defense on the roof, some means of escape. It didn't seem likely. He heard the people, far back in the house, pounding down the rooftop stairwell. "That *thing* isn't Kitty, and that isn't my mother either! In life, Kitty was a little broken, but those...things...are something else entirely! What *are* they?"

"You're right, John. Come along." They stepped inside. The floor squished and buckled under their weight; it was soaked through with kerosene. The oily fumes in the air made John gag. "These aren't the people that they resemble," Lenore continued, pulling John forward. "They're just...*dolls*. They don't *think*. They act out their anger and construct horrible scenes intended to...terrorize us. Mostly, they only remember the final offences that we wrought upon them, repeating actions and saying words that happened before we killed them."

Lenore rushed to the main stairwell and pried off one of the loose posts. "Grab a weapon, John." John went to the stairwell, but didn't find any more balusters that could be pulled off in time. All eight angry victims suddenly burst out of the door to the rooftop stairs onto the second floor, having come down the stairs from the roof. They held their weapons and rushed along the upstairs hallway toward the main stair. "Dolls, with no minds of their own," John said with disgust, "whose only purpose is to torture us."

Lenore nodded, just as the ring of flaming trees slammed into the house. She said, "Apologize to them, lie down before them, pray to them, pray *for* them, or try to give them a hug. I have tried it all. It makes no difference."

The victims were almost at the top of the stairs, approaching fast, in a big clump. John stepped to the entryway and grabbed the only thing nearby, one of the dusty old books from the nearest shelf. It was the Platonicus book that Lenore had talked to him about that one night by the fire.

Lenore looked down and, though the situation was dire, she smiled. "Oh, you're going with the 'really heavy book' option?"

Every window, every door, every possible exit was blocked by dense, burning trees, and the house caught fire right away. Lenore said, "When they attacked you in the basement a little while ago, they weren't necessarily trying to kill you; that was all just to torment and trouble you. But now, they will *end* us, no matter what. We must do whatever we need to, to them, to get to the roof." The group of eight victims ran down toward them, the warehouse worker in the lead. Lenore squared herself and said, "Hurting them now, killing them again, is irrelevant." She swung her weapon at the warehouse worker, knocking him in the shoulder. "No matter what we do here, John...they will just keep coming back." The little boy came at her, his face burning with hatred, his hands outstretched in grasping claws. "They may look like people, but they are shells, filled only with a lust for vengeance." She knocked the boy back, but he came again. "Remember, my love...they are *not alive*. You and I are the only real ghosts here."

Behind them, the entire first floor was completely ablaze. The little boy again flew at Lenore, as John's mother closed to strike as well, and Lenore grabbed the little boy by the hair, and used his momentum to throw him roughly down the stairwell. He bounced along the balusters and disappeared into the first floor fire. John's mother screamed and stabbed Lenore in the arm with the letter opener, but Lenore elbowed her away with the other arm.

John ducked under a swing from Rooster and hit the tall man in the side of the head with the heavy old book. As he moved further up the stairs, Kitty was right there, and she was ready. She slammed him solidly in the left collarbone with the axe, burying it so deep that part of the blade came out through John's back. John collapsed, staggering backwards and dropping the book, pulling the axe from Kitty's hands, losing ground all the way to the middle of the stairs, and nearly tumbling into the rising flames.

John looked down at the axe sticking out of his shoulder, and then down to the torn book, which was open nearby. Atop the printed writings of Platonicus, someone had drawn tiny, vertical hash marks, in groups of five, with the fifth stroke going diagonally across the other four. Both of the open pages were covered in these tight tally marks; there were thousands of strokes visible on just the two open pages that John could see.

Lenore moved toward John, and as the rest of the mob set upon her, she dodged the matron's large knife and smacked the red-faced woman in the head with her baluster club. She then skillfully swung it down to trip The Master, whose gigantic bulk fell into the others and gave Lenore an opening to get to John. She said, "Hold still, my love," and yanked the axe from his bloody shoulder. John could not move his left arm, but she shoved the axe into his right hand. "Now, fight!" she shouted, and they battled their way to the top of the stairs. The flames reached the second floor, where the carpets around them began to blaze. They hopped over this growing hazard, moving to the rooftop stairway. Lenore swung around nimbly, planting the post into the skull of The Master, who had recovered and was leading a new charge.

John shouted over to Lenore, "What is on the roof...is it a way out?"

The Master fell backwards into the portrait of himself at the top of the stairs, knocking it from the wall. The entire rectangular space behind it was covered with more tightly-grouped hash marks.

The old innkeeper dodged around The Master's falling bulk, and John hit her in the face with the blade of the axe. The second floor was fully ablaze, flames now licking at John's pants. Lenore said, "No, there's no way out. We will die here." John kicked the tiny, brittle body of the innkeeper away, further tripping up the remaining attackers as they neared. Lenore and John were able to make the bottom of the rooftop stairway, which itself was burning, and ran through the flames up to the top. As they made it to the roof, Lenore said, "By not letting them burn us up, I feel like we *win*, just a little." She slammed the rooftop door shut, and she and John leaned their bodies back against it as the mob below crashed into it on the other side. Lenore smiled over at him, as if this was all just another pleasant morning by the parlor fire. "You *do* know that we'll go around again, right? I'll know what I know, but you will remember none of this."

The letter opener still protruded from one of her arms. John's white shirt was a red mess, and his left arm hung limply from his shoulder. He could not move his hand. He and Lenore continued to press back against the door, holding it closed against the attackers who snarled and shouted on the other side. The door became hot against his back, as well as the rooftop on which he sat. Lenore continued, speaking calmly, "It's no guarantee that we end up like this, you know, here, in the house, making our stand on the roof. If I don't try hard enough, you go charging off into the mist and die within a week of re-gaining your strength! Or you end up hating me for all the terrible truths that I *know* but can't tell you...or you force me to tell you what I know, and it ends after a few weeks."

The mob continued slamming on the door, as the door itself started to burn from the bottom. The roof itself began to smoke and smolder.

"But I have gotten better and better at this, with practice, and *they* haven't changed at all. Our victims always perform the same torture play, with just a few variations, and I have become an expert at predicting how you will react, for the most part. I have changed this whole script, to something slightly happier."

John's head rocked forward from a particularly solid blow on the burning door behind them. He asked, "How many times have we been through it?"

Lenore sighed. "Thousands, I'm sure. Hundreds of thousands. I lost count and started to tally each pass, behind paintings, in books. Except for the Cartwright doll remembering what we ordered—but of course never giving it to us—those marks are the only thing that persists each time." She nodded, steeling herself for what needed to come next. "Please get ready, John. Will you take the final leap with me?"

The door behind them was breaking, and being pushed open. The Master's fat arm started to edge through the gap. Kitty's son scratched and grabbed at John's ruined shoulder through a burnt-out area of the door. "Yes," he said. "Have you figured out what the point is?"

"They want to burn us up here, in the ultimate torment, shredding our emotions and our bodies eternally...and, oh, I participated for the first thousand times or so. But nothing changed, no matter how sorry I was...and I am truly sorry. I'm sorry that I killed your mother and father, and the others."

"Me, too," John said sincerely. "I'm sorry that I killed your daughter and your grandson...and the others, too. My life was unremarkable, but I didn't really hurt anyone, until the very end. And even that was a terrible accident. Why do I deserve this?"

Lenore smiled, pulling the letter opener from her arm and casually stabbing it at the hands and arms that grasped at them from behind the burning rooftop door. "Before I killed her, didn't your mother teach you that killing is wrong?"

John laughed. "Good point. So what was that part about *me* not being any more of a murderer than *you*?"

"Think about it," she said, shrugging. "We each killed four people, so you are truly no more of a murderer than me. I try not to lie, but I *do* misdirect. Sometimes you need the right kind of encouragement."

His shoes and pants were burning, and the mob started to claw at him through the broken lower portion of the door. Below them, they saw John's horse, running away on the other side of the river.

"What of His Majesty?" John asked. "Is he a doll, too?"

"No, just a horse, as far as I can tell. And a bad-tasting one, at that."

John winced at the thought, and chuckled. He and Lenore stood up, still leaning against the remains of the door. John stomped on his mother's hand, which had been grabbing at his burning pant-leg.

"Look, John," Lenore said quickly. "They made a mistake when they formed this Hell. There can be *love* here...why is that even allowed? This isn't a horror story, or a tragedy where the girl loses the boy and everything ends in sadness! I choose to see this as a love story...where the girl fights against long odds to win the boy's heart, over and over and over. It's glorious!"

John smiled, and took her hand with his good hand. They were both burning.

"This isn't Hell, John, it's Heaven. You'll never grow old. You'll never rot in the ground. You'll never know *nothing*. We live forever! And we have *love*. Let's finish it, together. This next pain will be flecting, I promise. And I will see you again, my love, in just a few days!"

John nodded, and then they kicked away from the grasping hands holding them and ran, hand in hand, through the now-high flames, toward the edge of the burning roof. The door behind them burst open, and all eight angry victims tumbled out to the roof. Every part of Everbridge Manor was aflame.

They leapt off together, rocketing to the burning ground below, where the brittle rosemary bushes had once been. Their blazing clothes trailed flames behind them. When they hit, they each saw a single, brilliant flash of red, and then blackness.

Epilogue

Lenore stood in the front garden amidst the trampled rosemary bushes. Everbridge Manor loomed behind her, no longer burning, and back in the condition that it was in on the night when she killed four people and first jumped off the roof.

The sky was a muddy confusion of dark clouds. River's Edge still had two plumes of smoke lazily rising from the sites of her and John's crimes.

Lenore considered her preparations: making room in the downstairs storage room for John to recuperate, bringing a bed from the upstairs to the downstairs, boiling the roots and leaves needed to make the healing ointment for his wounds. She needed to make another tally mark in a book; this would be the last one that would fit in Platonicus, and next time she would have to pick another one in which to document future iterations. She would again pick those same hateful, tasteless green beans and carrots and would again split the same firewood for the months ahead. If she had known that this was how it would all turn out, she would have chopped some logs into firewood before going in and killing herself.

She thought about the very first time she had "come back" after dying. It was very confusing. After killing so many people in town on that fateful night, so, so long ago...and handing little John off to the matron, jumping off the roof and presumably dying, Lenore had found herself simply standing right in this same spot. She couldn't understand why she had *not* died—she wanted *so much* to die—and she had walked into the house right away, ignoring the lack of people in the entryway, up to the roof, and jumped off a second time. The same result happened. And she did it again. Each time, she felt the painful impact, saw the blinding red flash, the blackness...and then she showed up in the same spot. Dying *hurt*, and it was not long before Lenore realized that this was the point that this world was trying to make to her.

After that, on that third time around, it didn't take long before The Master attacked her in the night, a terrifying encounter where he painfully beat her to death. And she returned again, back to the front of the manor as if she had not just died.

When she found a way to survive the random attacks from all four of her victims, Lenore eventually lasted long enough to meet John, hauled by his horse across the Everbridge with his injuries from the fateful night where he, too, had killed four people...and of course, on that night he had his head stomped, to severe effect. Lenore did not know who he was, but nursed him back to health and, through conversation, discerned facts that John himself didn't even know: this was the *same boy*, the same John, who had watched her kill everyone in the office in River's Edge, but now he was a grown man. One night, before John was fully recovered, he was attacked in the downstairs hallway by Rooster and killed, at which point the strange, jelly-jar vessels all broke, and the burning trees had trapped Lenore inside the house, where she burned alive. Supremely painful, and definitely the point, she knew. And again, back to the rosemary bushes.

Around and around she went, trying to atone for her crimes, and also learning more each time about what this world—this Hell, she now knew to call it—would throw at her. After being torn apart emotionally and physically, and watching the same happen to John, over and over and over, Lenore eventually realized that no contrition would ever be enough. After a thousand deaths, she started to tally them in various places, but also started to try to manipulate the sequence. Nothing ever really changed. She got to the point where she knew what she could and could not say, and she could help John enough to prevent the destruction of all the vessels for a long time indeed. Eventually, no matter what happened, he would gain back his memories and end the sequence, but there was less pain, all around, if she took certain steps.

Providing too much information to John or manipulating him too much would end things more quickly, and yet too little information also posed a problem. John would only stay at the manor for so long, enduring painful attacks and unexplained mysteries, before charging off to one of the two destinations across the bridge. Lenore discovered the sequences that maintained life at the manor at a delicate balance. It was painful to allow it, but sometimes leaving John to find his own way through a confrontation was the best approach.

She kept waiting for Hell to change, to get *worse* based on her efforts to make things better. Dying was never fun, but, overall, the daily punishments never really varied. The house and grounds could move things, make things disappear or appear, make candles or lamps light or extinguish, as needed to ratchet up the pressure. Books flew from shelves of their own volition, and the scarecrow could appear next to them in bed or float down the hallway, as needed to terrify John or Lenore. The world could also produce frightening noises to fit a given scene of torment, such as the clanging of the hallway clock, screams in another room, warning vibrations, taps on the glass jars, or the sound of a body falling...but it was all just stage-dressing. The bizarre jelly jars in the basement "tracked" where they were in the overall sequence, magically smashing after John figured one of the puzzles out, always slowly increasing their unease, and the danger level in the house.

The dolls mostly did the same things over and over, essentially trying to terrorize them in the flavor of John's "haunted corn maze," but it was less scary if you knew where to expect the surprises. They seemed to have preferences, too: Rooster hit John with the double-hand clap, and Kitty loved to plug John with the axe, which she did regularly. Her boy gleefully staged John's horse in strange places, such as the roof or upstairs hallway, to confuse and annoy them.

The dolls usually reenacted things they did around the time they died, such as the matron falling to a heart attack or Rooster assaulting John...but sometimes they acted through angry scenes that had *nothing* to do with their previous lives. Kitty's little boy had never burned words in the walls or arranged to push someone into burning flames before, as far as Lenore knew, but he did that here, presumably because it was terrifying and confusing and painful. John succumbed to those flames many times before Lenore learned to intervene. Had the matron smashed cookware in the kitchen at any point in her real life, she would have been fired, or possibly beaten...but here, she acted this way to unnerve and frighten Lenore and John. There were only so many approaches to tormenting them, however, so all of these scenes inevitably repeated. With all of the repetitions, Lenore was able to slowly chart a different course through the most unpleasant obstacles.

And John was strong. That made Lenore's work here much

easier. He recovered from his injuries and was usually able to fight for himself to keep the dolls from ending him, even if he didn't understand why it was all happening. Lenore could not stay right by John's side the whole time; *that* scenario never played out for very long because it aroused all of John's suspicions far too early. So instead, she gave him some space, which meant that John frequently had to fend for himself in terrible situations. Thankfully, his military training and general fitness kept him alive through most of the early encounters.

Lenore was not always perfect in her actions. Sometimes, the emotional toll became too much for her, and she despaired. Sometimes, she failed to predict something John or the dolls would do...and one or both of them died, restarting the sequence. The cycle never lasted for more than one hundred days, no matter what Lenore tried. There was no rest in sleep either; her crimes repeatedly endlessly, painfully, in her dreams, as if each murder was occurring again, the first time. Lenore could usually look away from the painful scenes enacted in the manor itself, or River's Edge, but she could not escape the tremendous torment of the reenactments that happened in her dreams.

She counted the weeks until the sun broke free of the ever-present clouds, each time, for just one glorious minute. Her only explanation for this glimpse of the beautiful heavens was that the world wanted to show them a fleeting glimpse of amazing beauty, and then take it away because they were murderers who didn't deserve splendor. And she could calculate when Cartwright would come, promising to bring them what they wanted but never delivering. Again, the world said that she and John did not deserve the foods they asked for... they, in fact, did not deserve any tasty food at all.

Living with John through all of these repetitions, seeing the type of man he was, watching him try to help her—even though she was an often-deceptive stranger to him—Lenore started to fall in love with him. He never remembered anything when the sequence started again, which made sense, because at least one of them needed to forget all of it for the scenario to work as a continual torture. Though John forgot everything, *she* remembered everything, and she started to enjoy encouraging him to fall in love with her.

So that is what she did, honing her script each time, drawing as much pleasure for the two of them as she could manage. She was in Hell, but she could look past that as much as possible, and instead try to get John to fall in love with her. She never got tired of it.

This time, Lenore turned to head into the house, and stopped short. The giant blue swirl of light was back again, behind the outhouse, but closer to the house than it had been before. She saw glimpses of the strange eyes, in the dirt all around, as if tendrils of some strange beast had emerged from the blue swirl and its eyes were watching her. Since nothing ever really changed at the manor, Lenore was not sure what this blue creature was, but she had an idea: she thought it was her Maker, the one who had made this Hell and condemned her to it. For some reason, the Maker had come to observe her.

She didn't take the axe from the nearby stump and run, raging, at the blue swirl, as she had done on its previous appearance. She did not try to stomp on the eyes when she saw them. Instead, she just left it be, waiting to see what would happen. Of course, she had a lot to say to the Maker, should He ever present Himself for a chat, but she held those conversations inside herself waiting for the right time to give Him a piece of her mind.

Lenore went about her preparations, and eventually John and His Majesty strode across the bridge, to her delight and dismay. She disliked the anxious time before his arrival; she was comforted when they were together.

She nursed John back to some semblance of health, all

the while seeing the strange, flitting eyes on the ground outside, and even sometimes on the floors or walls of the manor itself; they never stayed still or stayed around anywhere for more than a few seconds at a time. On the night that Rooster and his nasty son ganged up on John in the hallway, burning their foul message into the walls and pushing John into the flames, Lenore became enmeshed in a protracted battle with John's mother. This battle between the two women occurred upstairs, in Lenore's room. Lenore spared no violence against the empty beings that attacked her and John; she knew they were vacant, torture dolls, but sometimes it took time to vanquish them. And occasionally, even though she mostly knew what would happen, they wounded or killed Lenore during their brawls. A delay and a grave wound happened on that night, when John's mother stabbed Lenore in the calf with the letter opener before retreating, slowing Lenore from rescuing John from the fire by patting it out with a blanket.

After John died, the jars broke and the trees came, and Lenore quickly pitched herself from the gables to avoid burning up.

When she found herself alive again, in front of the house, Lenore noticed that the blue swirl had moved closer. It was now in the middle of the main courtyard, ten feet from the front door. Lenore addressed it. "Have you seen enough? Do you have the nerve to come talk to me?" There was no response, but again, the eyes appeared all around the ground and the manor walls, and Lenore often felt watched as she played through the sequence and happily nursed John back to health. John was particularly confused about the giant, inexplicable blue phenomenon outside the front door, and struggled to believe anything Lenore told him. Few of her tricks worked, and John eventually got on His Majesty, rode down the Junction City road, found the end of the world, and presumably suffocated there. The cycle ended, and Lenore stood in her starting position, ready to try again.

This time, the giant blue swirl was in the front entryway, rising through a gigantic hole in the manor's roof, again touching the grey sky above. Strangely, most of the books in the house were gone, which Lenore found particularly confusing. As the days passed, she answered John's questions about this in-home wonder as best as she could, and they were able to run her script all the way through beyond Cartwright's useless visit, when he showed up without the strange twin in evidence. Lenore's luck continued further, culminating in two luxurious nights together with John in bed in the camp outside the house, to their great delight. After the discovery of the second murder site, John agreed that he loved her, which thrilled her heart every time...but he still rode off. Next, he returned from the edge of the world, wisely lashed to his horse, and the pair of them fought their perilous fight, past the swirling blue wonder up the two stairways to their eventual, shared decision to jump off together and try again.

WHEN LENORE RETURNED to her starting spot in the broken rosemary bushes, she noticed many changes in the landscape before her, and it made her gasp. Besides the appearance of the blue swirl several iterations ago, nothing—*nothing*—ever changed at Everbridge Manor.

But now, all of the spindly trees had been replaced, somehow, with the oddest variety of growing tree-like plants she had ever seen. There wasn't a single tree that had *green* leaves on it, but so many other colors were surprisingly in evidence: a group of trees with bright-red fronds grew behind the outhouse, and the whole forest on the other side of the lake was a combination of blue leaves, yellow leaves, and orange leaves. Many of the trees had strange-looking protuberances growing on them, as if they were fruit or flowers, but again, their colors and shapes were wilder than anything Lenore had ever observed, either in her real life before she came to this Hellish place, or after.

The blue swirling entity was not in the courtyard or entry-way; it was nowhere to be seen. The sky was as it always was, grey and foreboding.

Lenore gasped again when she saw Cartwright walking across the Everbridge. He walked up to her, smiling, and greeted her, "Hello, Lenore." She noticed immediately that it was the strange Cartwright-twin, the one with the eyeballs just visible inside his shirt, though with none of the awkward body-movements that he had demonstrated the first time she encountered him.

She was sure that this individual was a manifestation of the swirling blue entity that had been observing her for the last several loops. He had apparently mastered some amount of speech, as well as control of the Cartwright-shaped body that he was inhabiting. Further, she believed that this was her Maker, the one who had constructed this punishment land-scape for her and for John, and this made her angry. She had much to say to this individual, but didn't care to waste time doing it. She desperately wanted her life, her life in service of this continual, useless punishment, to end, permanently.

Her heart began pounding, very fast. "Do you have the power to end this?"

He was taken aback, but replied, "Why yes, I do. Why do you—"

She stepped closer, got right up in his face, and said, "Great! Please do it. Right now."

He said, "But Lenore—" and she interrupted him. She said, "Wait. Before you end it, let me tell you this: this Hell is a complete failure. Paying for the same sins over and over, for all eternity...it's ridiculous." She was getting worked up, breathing heavily, facing her tormenter and the blissful possibility of having it all stop. Eternal rest seemed to her like the greatest kind of blessing. "Doing anything," she continued, "...forever... even *pleasure*...even your promise of eternal joy in heaven makes no sense at all. Now. End it."

The man who looked like Cartwright stepped back and said, "Lenore, I believe you have me confused with someone else. I did not make this place. I just 'discovered' it, and came closer to learn what was happening here." His manner of speech was clipped and strange. He said the word "discovered" with a specific emphasis that made Lenore imagine quotation marks around the word, as if he was trying hard to emphasize his new ability to use the "right" words in her language.

"What do you mean, 'discovered' it? What exactly are you?"

"Your language doesn't have words to describe my kind, or even to pronounce my name. I know this, because I checked— reading all of the 'sacred texts' in your manor to learn your tongue, and listening to all of your conversations. But understand that I am an 'explorer,' and also a 'creator'...possibly like this 'Maker' you mistook me for."

Lenore was undeterred, as the prospect of relief finally presented itself. "Fine. That's all very surprising, really, but if you have the ability to end this, I beg you to do it."

Cartwright said, "I'm sure you do, after what I have seen here. Much of it doesn't make 'sense' to me still, but I understand enough to know that this world is '*wrong*.'"

"Agreed," Lenore said. "This is all so very 'wrong.' Please clap your hands, or whatever it is you need to do, to make it go away. Why can't I just *die*, as was so regularly foretold during my first, real life?"

"But I have not yet shown you all that I wish to show you. As I said, I am a creator, but, unfortunately, I cannot re-make the civilization from which you supposedly came, nor anything even remotely like it. What I can make for you 'from scratch' would probably scare you, to be honest." He pointed to the strange trees all around. "But this vegetation is something that I re-created from a world on the other side of the universe, and it has what you would call 'vegetables' and 'fruit' that can sustain you. Some of these 'trees' are strong enough to be used for building, as well, should you wish to build 'additional structures.' This world still has the same boundaries it had before, but I covered the whole area outside the manor grounds with various types of useful vegetation. I thought you would like this, as well: the town of River's Edge is no longer there at all."

Lenore said, "Good riddance," but she was still unimpressed. She had no desire to build any "additional structures," instead hoping more for a "quick exit." She had experienced enough living, and dying, for so, so many lifetimes.

Cartwright continued, "Another thing I can do, is to '*eliminate*' things. I have eliminated all of the 'torture dolls,' as you called them. They will never return. When you sleep, you will have no 'bad dreams.' And I put a 'rock' in the space where your basement used to be, so there is no chance of a fire from the jars that were once there."

Lenore was cheered by the idea of Everbridge Manor without its vicious residents, without the ticking bomb that had been in the basement, but she was still tired of living here. "Thank you for making these changes, but I would truly welcome an end to all of this. I am ready. Please 'eliminate' this world."

Her strange visitor was undeterred. "Hold on. I can also '*rearrange*' things that happen here, such as: this." The black clouds above swirled for a few moments, forming a familiar localized tornado above the grounds, and then all of them dissipated. A flawless blue sky remained, stretching in all directions. The sun blazed gloriously above, warming Lenore's face, which she turned upward with a serene smile. She laughed and said, "Sunshine!"

They looked at the sky silently for a while, and then Cartwright said, "This place always had a functioning representation of a day-star and a night-moon. They were just covered up with those 'clouds.'"

Lenore waited more than minute to see if the beautiful sky remained, and it did. As exquisite as it was, however, she was still unconvinced. The depth of her previous torment was too much, and she still craved the real end. "Thank you for letting me see this, one last time. You are so generous, truly...but I have endured so much pain—"

Cartwright held up one hand. "I believe I understand your reluctance to continue existing, Lenore. In addition to using your books to learn your 'language,' I also used them to quantify the tally marks you made in them. The resulting count is two very high numbers."

"How do you mean, two high numbers?"

"The total value is two thousand, and nine hundred."

Lenore thought about this, and scoffed. "Less than three thousand times? That can't be right. I have shot myself with my Grand-daddy's rifle, at least that many times."

"Well, it is two zero zero zero, nine zero zero. Do you not say that as—"

"You mean two *million* and nine hundred. Yes, that certainly seems right." She paused a moment, considering, and said, "Let me ask you this: why have you come to *my* Hell? Why not look in on all the *other* Hell's, or even on the real world where I used to live?"

"Your 'Hell,' as you call it, is the only thing in this region of space. A bubble of light in a sea of darkness. There are no planets or stars or moons, no life at all, anywhere near this place. That is what attracted my attention."

"Well, I really appreciate you coming to call on me, and all of these astonishing gifts," Lenore said, pointing to the blue sky and the robust trees all around. "...but alas, I must go."

Cartwright nodded. "If you wish it, Lenore. I know of your pain. But as I said, I can 'rearrange' things, and there is one more thing you should see."

A horse walked onto the far side of the Everbridge, with an unconscious, wounded man precariously balanced on the saddle. Only a few tangles of the reins kept him from falling to the wooden planks of the bridge.

Lenore whispered, "Oh...John," and stumbled forward onto one knee, suddenly crying. Cartwright helped her up, and she ran over to the horse and touched John's bleeding face. He opened his eyes, just a little, and asked, "Kitty?"

Lenore's body shuddered with joyful sobs, and tears ran down her face. She said, "No, my love, I'm Lenore."

Cartwright walked over to them and asked Lenore, "Will you stay?"

Lenore whispered, "How long will we have?"

"'Forever,' if you wish. Or as long as this bubble of life persists, which will be a very long time."

Lenore shook her head firmly. "No. It *must* end, truly. Not right away, but at some point. Nothing that lasts forever makes any sense at all."

Cartwright nodded, and said, "I must rest, after effecting these changes. If you wish, I can return in fifty of your years."

Lenore grabbed the reins of the horse, leading it toward the front of the manor. "That's fine. But don't come to visit us when you return, just turn the whole thing off...from space, or wherever it is you come from."

"Since that will be the first time you really die," Cartwright observed, "perhaps there will be something *after*, as foretold in many of your 'sacred texts.'"

"Don't go starting that up again!" Lenore said tersely, wiping away her tears. "One life, followed by eternal rest...that is a vast, unexpected gift. Be sure to end it, as you've promised."

"Shall I not see you again?"

"No, just wait for us to have a life together…fifty years is fine, a magnificent treasure, for which I thank you…and then *turn it off*. I don't care if we're in the middle of a sentence, or if we just took a bite of your colorful fruit. Please end it."

Cartwright said, "As you wish." He stepped away, and the air around him shimmered, and in the next instant he was back to his whirling, blue, funnel-form. He shot up into the beautiful sky above, and was gone.

Lenore touched John's cheek, which was swollen and cut, but which she knew would heal.

"Come along, John. I know just what to do."